"Mary, Mary," he whispered.

"Never contrary." She closed her eyes and inhaled the spicy scent of sage and wood smoke.

Logan hooked his arm behind her head, opened his mouth over hers and stole her next breath with the kiss she wanted, the kind that gave back and kept on giving. She welcomed him, her tongue touching his, her lips taking the measure of his. Full and moist, they took the lead in a sexy slow dance meant to bring more dancers to the floor, meant to get things going up and down their bodies, bundles of nerves dying to become entangled in utterly wild ways. In the end he touched his forehead to hers, and they mixed breath with breath and sigh with sigh.

He lifted his head. "Would you like to stay with me tonight?"

ou/ri91 Hit

Dear Reader,

What animal do you associate with romance?
For me, it's the horse. Whether he's a knight in shining
armor or a cowboy in well-worn blue jeans, my heroes
ride horses. It's no surprise that I fell in love with
my own Indian cowboy during a summer filled with
horseback rides across miles of rolling prairie.

So join us under the vast South Dakota sky for
the story of a man and a woman who come from
two very different worlds that are "just down the road"
from each other. What brings them together? The
Double D Wild Horse Sanctuary and a competition for
horse trainers. Logan Wolf Track is "the best there is,"
and so is Sergeant Mary Tutan. But Mary trains dogs.
This is a story about neighbors becoming friends, friends
becoming lovers, and families built on love.

Once again, come with me to a place where wildness
reigns and love conquers all.

All my best, always,

Kathleen Eagle

ONCE A FATHER

KATHLEEN EAGLE

Silhouette®

SPECIAL EDITION®

Published by Silhouette Books

America's Publisher of Contemporary Romance

To Honor the Memory of
Barbara Eagle

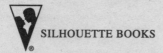

SILHOUETTE BOOKS

ISBN-13: 978-0-373-65548-9

Recycling programs
for this product may
not exist in your area.

ONCE A FATHER

Copyright © 2010 by Kathleen Eagle

Visit Silhouette Books at www.eHarlequin.com

Printed in U.S.A.

KATHLEEN EAGLE

published her first book, a Romance Writers of America Golden Heart Award winner, with Silhouette Books in 1984. Since then she has published more than forty books, including historical and contemporary, series and single title, earning her nearly every award in the industry. Her books have consistently appeared on regional and national bestseller lists, including the *USA TODAY* list and the *New York Times* extended bestseller list.

Kathleen lives in Minnesota with her husband, who is Lakota Sioux. They have three grown children and three lively grandchildren.

Author Note

This story is set in southwestern South Dakota, near the Black Hills on a Lakota (Sioux) reservation. I have purposely not tied the story to a specific reservation, but I have made every effort to portray Lakota culture accurately.

If you're a horse lover like me, check out the Black Hills Wild Horse Sanctuary online at www.wildmustangs.com. Douglas O. Hyde founded the program in 1988, and it is the inspiration for the Double D Wild Horse Sanctuary.

Chapter One

The barefaced loner with the long, brown hair and the distance runner's body was a woman apart. She was no fence-sitter, no small-talker, no crowd-joiner. She had come for the horses and nothing else.

Logan Wolf Track liked her already.

He would likely change his mind before the day was over but being drawn to her at first sight counted for something. His hard-earned instincts rarely failed him. He knew a kindred spirit when he saw one. Whether he could work with her, kindred or otherwise, was something else. Twenty thousand dollars worth of something else, he told himself as he approached the woman.

He had come for the horses *and* the money.

South Dakota's Double D Wild Horse Sanctuary was filled to capacity with horses the Bureau of Land Management had placed in the care of sisters Sally Drexler and Ann Drexler Beaudry, but the horse-loving women—particularly Sally—were hell-bent on making room for more. A bottleneck in the BLM's wild horse adoption program—plenty of adoptees, few adopters—had the ever-resourceful Sally coming up with a plan for every letter in the alphabet.

Logan wanted in on her latest production. Thanks to Ann's rich brother-in-law, Sally had found a sponsor for "Mustang Sally's Makeover Challenge." Trainers had three months to show the world that wild horses could be made into excellent mounts. The reward had Logan's name written all over it. Not only the cash, but the cachet. His way with horses was like no one else's, and he'd written a book on the subject. Not that he'd sold many copies, but that didn't mean it wasn't a great book. All his training method needed was a little publicity, and winning Sally's contest could bring him that.

Unfortunately, Sally had thrown him a curve.

In the shape of an hourglass.

"Did they turn you down?" he asked the woman's back. He knew her first name, but she would have to give it to him before he'd use it. She was watching a dozen young horses chase each other around in a holding pen. Another handful had just been released into a nearby pasture, which put the captives in a tizzy.

The woman turned and drilled him with a look. Killer eyes. She knew it, too. She held Logan's gaze long enough to let him know he'd interrupted something. Then she looked down at the crumpled paper in his fist.

"Sally's right. I'm not qualified to train a wild horse." She looked up. That quickly the color of her eyes had gone from icy gray to cool blue. "It sounds really exciting, but realistically, I don't have that much time." She squinted against the sun. "What about you?"

"I'm too qualified." Logan gave half a smile. The woman wore a reserved expression on a pleasing face. No makeup, no pretense, nothing fancy. A good face, easily read. Her time in the sun had not been spent on the beach. She took care of herself, but pampering was not on her schedule. And she kept a schedule. "Sally tried to pull some *conflict of interest* excuse on me, but I know better."

The woman tipped her head to the side, genuinely curious, still squinting. Logan's straw cowboy hat shaded his face. He had the advantage. He could see her just fine. "What are you interested in?" she asked.

"Training horses. But I'm on the Lakota Tribal Council—Lakota Sioux—and I guess you could say we're supporting Sally's training competition in a roundabout way. We just decided to lease a bunch more land for the wild horse sanctuary. It's true I talked it up and voted for it." He turned to watch the horses. "But I still don't see it. The Tribe isn't putting up prize money or judges, nothing like that."

"If she's gonna be that picky, she won't have anyone competing." She turned, too. They stood side by side, nearly shoulder to shoulder, sharing a common disappointment. "I train dogs," she reported.

He knew that. He suspected he had the advantage there, too. On the heels of his rejection, Sally had pointed the woman out to him through the office window. His wasn't the only application she couldn't approve, but she hated to turn good people down flat. Where there was a will, there might be a way.

"If you're good at it, that's experience in my book," Logan allowed. "Which one do you like?"

"That one." She pointed to a gelding the color of river water. His dark mane, tail and dorsal stripe were signs that his mustang ancestry went way back. "He doesn't want to be here, any more than the rest of them, but he's here, and he'll deal with it intelligently. You can see it in his eyes."

"You think he's intelligent?"

"In his world he is. He'll take cues from someone who knows how to give them."

"What would you use him for?" He met her quizzical glance with more test questions. "That's what the competition is about, right? Making him useful?"

"I'd ride him. I'd gentle him so that a child could ride him."

"Do you have one in mind?" He glanced away. "A kid to show the horse at the end of the competition."

"I just meant he'd be that gentle. Gentle enough for anyone to ride." Her voice softened. "It's been a long time since I've been around children."

"Where's your dog?"

"Halfway across the world." She turned to him, shoulders squared, right hand his for the shaking. "Mary Tutan. *Sergeant* Mary Tutan, U.S. Army. Home on leave."

"Logan Wolf Track. Home to stay."

"Lucky you." Her hand slid away. He wasn't a shaker. In his world hands greeted without pressure, palm to palm. He liked her friendly smile. "Sally and I have been friends since we were kids, and I really love what she's doing here. Just so you know, whatever her side is, I'm on it." Her straight hair flew back from her face as she turned it into the soft summer wind. "That paint is nice, too. And I like the pretty red roan."

"You wanna win this thing, or not?"

She gave a quick laugh. "If I were in it, I'd be in it to win it."

"The paint's too narrow across the shoulders, and that roan is walleyed."

"*Wild*-eyed?"

"Same thing. In this case you're not lookin' to see the whites of their eyes. Same with dogs, right? All you wanna see in the eyes is color." Forearms braced on the fence rail, he glanced past his shoulder and met her studied gaze. She was taking mental notes. He nodded. "I like your first choice."

"Me, too. If wishes were horses, that's the one I'd ride."

"I can make that wish come true for you. If you're serious." Her eyes questioned him again. "Your friend Sally has something up her sleeve. Maybe you know what it is."

"An arm." She smiled. "Sally plays by the rules. She doesn't pull tricks. I'm sure she'd love to—"

"That's exactly what she said. She'd love to have me compete, but she wants me to take on a partner, and she strongly suggested you." *Surprised?* Check. Nothing up Mary Tutan's short, unrestricted sleeve. Open for further explanation. "You apply for the competition. You train the horse. I train you."

"She said that?"

Recalling his own reaction—less surprise, more irritation—Logan chuckled. "I think she's making up the rules as she goes along, which makes it easy to play by them if you're Sally. Thing is, I like Sally and I might just be willing to give her game a shot. How about you?"

She searched his face for signs of sense. "I only have thirty days."

"I have whatever it takes." He smiled. "And then some."

"That makes you an interesting man, Mr. Wolf Track."

"Logan."

"With an interesting proposition," she allowed, which surprised him. "But what's in it for you?"

He lifted one shoulder. "My regular fee or a share of the prize money, whichever way you wanna go."

"I doubt that I could afford your fee. And I wouldn't do it for the money." She turned her attention to the gelding. "I love horses."

"Perfect. You do it for love. I'll do it for money." She laughed. He didn't. "I'm serious."

"Yeah, well, I'm—"

"Sergeant Mary Tutan, who says she wishes she could ride that horse. I'm saying I can make your wish come true if you're willing to put the prize money where your mouth is." She stared. He smiled. "And I can do it in thirty days."

"What about the other sixty?"

"That's for the kid." She frowned, and he elaborated. "The one we're gonna get to show the horse."

"I can't. I'd love to, but I just…" Here it came. The backpedaling. "I really just came to see my mother. I can't stay. I don't know why Sally would suggest that you partner up with me." She hit a rock and stopped pedaling. "Something to do with my father?"

"I don't know your father."

"Dan Tutan? He has a ranch right up the road. He leases Indian land."

"You think I know every rancher who leases Indian land?" He glanced away. *A little disingenuous, there, Wolf Track.* Some of the tribal land Dan Tutan had been leasing was about to become part of the Double D Wild Horse Sanctuary. "I know who he is. That doesn't mean I know him. All I know about Sally's suggestion is that she vouches for you personally, and she thinks you'd like to, *love* to enter 'Mustang Sally's Makeover Challenge' but you need a horse trainer. I'm the best there is."

Mary stared at the house, shook her head and muttered, "Sally, Sally, Sally."

"So how about you fill out the papers and we get started?"

"Just like that?"

"You're the one who's only got thirty days."

She gave him one of those little head shakes peculiar to women. *I would, but there's this problem.* "I'd want to be able to show him myself, and I'm not the best rider."

"We'll train him for Western pleasure. I don't care who shows him."

"You want to win this thing or not?" she mimicked.

He shrugged. "We don't win, I get nothing. You give me the money, honey, I'll put in the time."

"What about the love?"

"That I can't help you with."

"You don't have to. I really would love to do this. It would be…" She crossed her arms and hugged herself. "I'm feelin' it already."

"Well, there you go."

"Where?" She leaned closer. "Where do I go? I mean, where would we do this? And how would we—"

He laid his hand on her shoulder. "You sign the papers and leave the rest up to me."

The Drexlers' rambling old house had long been a second home for Mary. As a girl she'd sometimes pretended it was her first home. And then she'd thought about Mother and mentally flagellated herself. Even with those days long gone, she entered the mudroom through the squeaky screen door and boxed those old, familiar feelings around. *Ah, yes, the door—oh, damn, it isn't mine.* She was greeted by a sweet yellow dog, ignored by an old calico cat.

"Come on in," called a beloved voice.

"It's me again," Mary called back as she signaled the dog to stay and the man to come.

"In the office, you again."

Mary led the way through sunny kitchen, comfy living room and dim foyer to present herself in the doorway to Sally's office-by-day, bedroom-by-night. She took a parade rest stance.

"Okay, girlfriend, just what *are* the rules for this contest you've got going here?"

Sally spun her ergonomically correct chair away from the computer desk and grinned. "I see you two found each other."

"Surprise, surprise. You said I wasn't qualified to enter, but then you told…" Mary stepped aside, ceding the doorway to her companion.

"Logan," Sally prompted, "that he couldn't have a horse because he's on the Tribal Council, and they lease us a lot of land for which we are enormously grateful. And I told him you're somebody who's interested in the challenge and might be able to get a horse, but you'd need to work with somebody who knows horses." Sally bounced her eyebeams between visiting faces. "Perfect Jack Sprat kind of a deal, don't you think?"

"I have to be in Fort Hood in thirty days."

"So, you'd be in Texas. It's not like you'd be on the moon. Not *quite*. I've got applications from as far away as…" Sally snatched a paper from one of three wire baskets—red, gray and green—on the corner of her desk. She adjusted her glasses and focused on the top of the page. "Here's one from New York. Now *that's* a different world. She says she lives on a reservation. Are there real Indians in New York?"

"All kinds," Logan said.

"Good. I want all kinds of distribution. Geographical, cultural, economic, the whole barbecued enchilada. Nothing like wild horses to drag in all kinds." Sally shot Mary a suggestive look. "Maybe they can drag you back from Texas on weekends."

"That wouldn't make a lot of sense." She had to hear herself say the sensible thing. One crazy indulgence—*possible* indulgence—was one more than her limit. "But right now…just so we're clear…"

"Like the woman said," Logan put in. "About those rules."

"There are rules, and then there are…considerations." Sally tossed the New York application aside. "I'm working with Max Becker out of the Bureau of Land Management's Wyoming office. He's the wild horse specialist there, and he helped me get the competition approved. We worked together on the application you both filled out. We don't want anyone crying foul and giving wild horse and burro protection a black eye. Any more budget cuts and the program will go from a shoestring to a single-thread operation."

"If we don't qualify, we don't qualify," Mary said.

"*Separately* you don't qualify. But I don't have a problem with the entrant getting help from an experienced trainer." Sally turned her eyeball-to-eyeball *considerations* from Mary to Logan. "And there's no reason the trainer can't be on the Tribal Council."

"Are you making this stuff up as you go along?" Logan sounded more bemused than troubled.

"When we get into the gray areas I'm making most of the calls. Max is pretty busy. Plus…" Sally gestured toward the baskets. "…qualified applications aren't exactly flooding in. See, these are my *'In'* boxes."

They were labeled *"Ifs," "Ands"* and *"Buts."*

"Which ones have been rejected?" Mary asked.

"Those." Sally pointed to a metal trash can. "What does the army call 'File Thirteen'?"

"They don't even get a rejection letter?"

"Annie's handling that end of it. She writes such nice letters, we even get donations back from some of the rejects."

"I haven't gotten any letter," Mary told Logan. "Have you?"

He shook his head. "Must be in the *'But'* pile."

"You're both *'Ifs.'* Together you could move from gray to green." The look in Sally's eyes went from that of woman on top to woman in love. Mary and Logan turned to see the cause.

Hank Night Horse stood in the doorway ready with a handshake for each. Mary's came with a cowboy salute—touch of a finger to the brim of the hat—and Logan got a slap on his shoulder. "How's it goin', Track Man?"

"Have you figured this woman out yet?" Logan asked jovially. "Which box are you in?"

Hank and Sally exchanged affectionate glances.

"No conflict of interest there," Logan said to Mary.

"No 'ifs', 'ands' or 'buts' about it." Mary stepped to one side.

"Just so we're clear, I'm not competing. I've got my hands full right now." And to prove it Hank crossed the room, planted himself on the window seat behind his woman and rested his big hands on her slight shoulders. "But this guy's the best there is, Sally. He'll have his horse telling jokes while you clear the ring for the next contestant."

"I don't do stunts," Logan said. "A horse is a horse."

"Of course, of course!" Sally chimed in. Giddiness looked good on her. "And I want you to do what you do so well. I want this competition to generate some wonderful stories. Like the one about the Lakota horseman and the warrior woman. That's going straight to *Horse Lover's Journal.*"

"Warrior woman," Mary echoed with a chuckle. "I guess that's better than 'dog soldier.'"

"Why?" Hank asked. "Dog soldiers were the Cheyenne's best warriors. Just lately they started up again. My sister got married to one, up in Montana. Anybody calls you a dog soldier, you take it as a compliment."

"I do. I'm good at my job, too, and I prefer 'dog soldier' to 'dogface' but canine specialist has a better ring to it."

"You don't wanna be called a whisperer?" Logan asked. "Everybody's whispering these days."

"Got that, cowboy?" Sally slid Hank a playful smile. "You whisper, I purr."

"I know."

"Sweet," Logan teased. "Rumor has it he can sing pretty good, too."

"I know," Sally said.

Mary looked at Logan and cocked an eyebrow. "You get the feeling we're in the way here?"

"I'll get out of the way when I get what I came for," he said. "You sign up for the horse, you got yourself a trainer."

She glanced at Sally, who beamed back at her. *Beaming you up, old chum.* They'd spent precious little time together since Mary had enlisted, but the years fell away instantly because Sally was…Sally.

No more sidestepping. No looking down. There was only the man at her side and the chance at hand. She looked him in the eye. "What's this gonna cost me?"

"A fair share of the prize."

"How much of a share?"

"Depends on what you contribute time- and effort-wise. You gonna pony up, Sergeant?"

With the help of some army training, Mary had learned to welcome a good challenge, especially when it came from a worthy challenger. "Half," she said. "Half is fair, and we split the expenses down the middle, win or lose."

"We can't lose. This is one of those win-win deals like you read about. Who's gonna write the story?"

"Which…?" Sally was so deep into their game she was practically falling out of her chair. The look of a sidelines fan suddenly hit with the ball carned her a laugh. Sally being Sally, she took it in stride. "Oh, we're gonna have all kinds of stories. That's the whole point. We need to get the word out about these horses." She glanced toward the door and smiled. "I think I'll put Annie in charge of that little detail."

"What little de— Mary!" Sally's younger sister surged into the room and greeted Mary with a hug. "Are you home for good? Stateside, at least? My God, you look wonderful."

"So do you." Smaller. Happier. How long had it been—five or six years? Oh, the nicknames she and Sally had hung on little Annie when they were kids. Chubby Cheeks. Mary glanced at the tall, dark and handsome cowboy trailing "Cheekers" and gave herself points for not blurting that one out. "This must be your new husband. Congratulations. I'm Mary Tutan."

Zach Beaudry offered a tentative hand. "Tutan? As in…"

"As in Damn Tootin's daughter."

"And my best friend forever," Sally said emphatically. "Dan Tutan has nothing to say about that."

"Oh, he has plenty to say. He's a difficult man, my father. Nobody knows that better than I do." Mary offered a shrug and sigh. "Nobody except my mother. And my brother." She gave an apologetic smile. "And our friends."

"We had a very small wedding," Ann said quickly. "At a lodge in the Black Hills. Very few guests. Mostly family." Ann had to reach up to put her arm around Mary's shoulders. "Of course, if you'd been here…"

"I don't blame you for not inviting him. If I were having a wedding, I wouldn't invite him either. He's…" Mary glanced at Logan. "…difficult."

"You know how he feels about the horses and the sanctuary," Sally said. "That's the problem."

"With my father it's not about feelings. It's about having things his way. That's what he lives for. His way puts food on the table, so that's a good thing. As long as you like to eat what he likes to eat."

There was an awkward silence. Mary let it play out, a buffer between revealing more than she meant to—not quite as much as she wanted to—and taking a deep breath of fresh Drexler air.

She turned to Logan. The challenge was more important to her now than it had been an hour ago. "How does half sound?"

"What are you willing to do for your half?"

"Learn. If you're as good as they say, I'm willing

to be your apprentice." She smiled. "I know how to take orders."

"I don't give orders. You watch and listen, maybe you'll learn from me, maybe not." He glanced at Sally, whose grin was all *atta boy*. He folded his arms and turned back to Mary. "So, what else?"

"Whatever needs doing."

He gestured toward Sally's wire baskets. "Staple us together and give us a horse."

Chapter Two

"Mother, what are you doing?" Mary hurried to Audrey Tutan's side and reached for the handle on the old ice cream freezer her mother had just carried upstairs. "This comes under the heading of heavy lifting, which is against the doctor's orders." It was the metal canister and hand crank inside the bucket that made the old turquoise contraption so heavy, and the steep stairway made the heavy lifting potentially fatal. Mary eased the load from her mother's hand, pulled the string dangling from the bare lightbulb and shut the door against the darkness.

"I thought we were taking some time off from orders," Mother said after catching a couple of breaths.

"Besides, that isn't so heavy, and your father has a sudden urge for homemade ice cream."

"If *we* aren't taking orders that includes *everybody's* orders." Mary lifted a warning finger. "Except your doctor's. I took notes, so don't even think about pushing your limit, which is a package of marshmallows. Did he tell you to make ice cream?"

"No, no, he just mentioned it. He remembers how you used to go crazy over homemade ice cream after you discovered Grandma's old ice cream freezer down in the basement. Haven't used it since you left home."

"They make electric..." Mary unloaded the 1960s dinosaur on the same vintage kitchen table and brushed her hands together. "You don't mean you've been rummaging around in the basement."

"Didn't have to. I knew right where it was. Beside, it's nice and cool down there. On the way back up the temperature seemed to rise five degrees for each step. I thought I'd make strawberry."

Mary eyed the old clunker. She hardly remembered Grandma, who had died when she was eight and was fondly remembered, especially for all the unwritten recipes she'd handed down to her daughter. Clearly Mother clung to some hope for her own daughter. *Into your hands I commend the mighty ice cream freezer.* She took the top off the metal canister and checked for debris. There was only the paddle she'd cleaned of ice cream more than once with her eager young tongue.

She'd use soap and water this time.

"They make smaller ones, too," Mary said absently as her mother took a large kettle from the cabinet above the stove. "Did he really say all that? *Let's have homemade ice cream for Mary?*"

"I know how he thinks."

Mary kept her doubts on that score to herself. Audrey Tutan had become a recluse since her children had left home. She'd always been a mind reader as far as Mary was concerned, but she'd been as protective of the cache in her daughter's head as she was of her own. The only tales she ever told were meant to promote peace in the Tutan household. What she could see inside her husband's head was anybody's guess. Steadfast and quiet, Mary's mother had always stood by her man. Just this once, could she step away and be with Mary?

Don't bring him into our conversation, Mother. Let me have your ear. Let me give you mine.

"How's Sally?" Audrey asked as she opened the refrigerator door.

"Sally Drexler has met her match. I've never seen her this happy."

"I've met him. He seems like a nice man, but does he…" Audrey turned, milk jug in hand. "Well, realistically, how's her health?"

"Realistically, multiple sclerosis is incurable,

Mother." *Don't hang your head, Mother. It's just you and me.* Mary checked the contents of the sugar canister before setting it within Audrey's reach. "I'm sorry. I didn't mean that the way it sounded. You were just asking."

Audrey wasn't ready for the sugar, but she laid her hand over the canister lid anyway. Mary touched the hand that once fed her, felt Mother's gratitude through cool, tissue-paper skin. The feel of fragility shook her to the core. Word from afar that her mother was in the hospital hadn't surprised her. She knew her duty. She took the leave, took the journey, took her place at her mother's side, and then, finally, it hit her. Her mother was mortal.

"She had her cane close at hand," Mary went on, "but she's full of Sally spunk. All excited about the competition they're running to get more people interested in wild horses. You enter up, you get to pick a horse and train it for whatever you want and show it at the end of the contest. Big cash prize for the winners. *Winner.* Whatever."

Mary opened a cupboard and took out measuring cups. She pulled a ring full of spoons from a reliable drawer. Mother's helper was a familiar role. Knowing the drill made for a comfortable segue from what they both knew to what one of them wanted to say and needed the other to hear. They could take turns. There was so much, and it was confusing and even if there were no answers it seemed as though the questions should be voiced.

What's going on with our bodies, Mother? You don't know? If you don't know, who does?

Disorder, that's what. One wonky part throws the whole system off, right? One misstep causes temporary tailspin. Take a deep breath and wait for the spinning to stop. Take the time to get everything in line. What Mary liked best about the army was order. Clarity. Why couldn't she bring the clarity home with her?

Home? What was that?

Start with something simple, Mary.

She leaned her hip against the edge of the counter. "I want to try it."

"Training a horse?" Audrey turned the burner on under the milk. "How long does that take?"

"You get ninety days."

"You mean…" Breathless pause. "…you're not going back?"

Was that hope or fear? It was hard to tell with Mother. Either way, Mary knew the feeling, and it was damn prickly. She lifted one shoulder. "I'd have a training partner."

"What are you talking about, girl?" Both women turned in the direction of the voice. "That dog food farm down the road?"

Speaking of prickly. Dan Tutan either stormed into a room or appeared out of nowhere. Either way, he enjoyed taking people off guard. He would have made a hell of a c.o., Mary thought. George Armstrong Tutan.

"I was talking to Mother."

"And I was joking with you, Daughter." Father's smile never touched his eyes. "I know the Drexler girls are your friends. I don't much like what they're doing over there, but since they're my girl's friends, they can raise all the dog food they want. I'll even borrow 'em my sausage grinder when it comes time to butcher." He raised an instructive finger. "That was another joke."

"Of course." *Who would have guessed?*

He moved in close enough to get a peek into the kettle. Audrey stepped to one side, stirring, stirring, stirring. Mary held her ground.

"You're not making vanilla, are you?"

"Strawberry," Audrey said.

"Good." He glanced at Mary as he turned away from the stove. "Why didn't you bring one of your dogs with you? Show me some of their tricks."

"They're working dogs."

"The army doesn't give them any leave time?" Her father chuckled.

"She sent us a wonderful training video," Audrey said as she tested the milk with her finger. "She's in it, working with the smartest dog I've ever seen." She flipped the burner off, glancing at Mary as she moved the kettle. "I watched it on the computer. He doesn't like computers."

"They don't like me."

"We should all watch it together," Audrey suggested. "Mary can tell us more than what they say on the video. I mean, more about what she actually does and how those dogs…" She rummaged in the refrigerator and backed out with eggs and cream. "We could have our ice cream while we watch, and I could pop some—"

"They're trying to take over that whole area west of the highway," Dan said, never one to let a bad joke go to waste. "All that Indian land I've been leasing over there."

"It's mostly badlands, isn't it?" Mary said. Part of her wanted to fall back and ignore his remarks, but the rest of her wanted to take a position and push back.

"Hell, no. There's a lot of grass out there, and the Tribe wants to turn it over to those girls and their welfare program for horses."

"You hardly use that land. It's as wild as those horses are."

"That's how much you know about cattle ranching. What's gonna happen to this place after I'm gone? Between you and your brother…." He drew a deep breath and blew out heated disgust. "You work your whole life to build something solid, and you want to be able to put your name on it and hand it over to heirs who know how to carry on. Born ranchers. Tutan heirs."

"Sounds like a group of backup singers," Mary quipped. "The Tutanaires."

"I could sure use some backup for a change. When it comes down to it—and sooner or later it will, between their horses and our cows—we'll see who's a Tutan heir. Between you and your brother…"

"You already said that. How long has it been since you heard from my brother?"

Silence. Her older brother had left home as soon as he'd finished high school. Mary admired him for putting himself through college and getting involved with the Forest Service in the Pacific Northwest. Sadly, she and Tom had allowed distance and the passage of time to get the better of their relationship.

"He called me on Mother's Day," Audrey said. "He and Adrienne are fine."

"Good to know," Mary said. "If he ever changes his mind about South Dakota, he's welcome to the place as far as I'm concerned."

"He has to change his mind about me first. Owes me—" Dan made a dismissive gesture "—an apology, to start with. After that, he owes me the two thousand dollars I loaned him to get himself a car."

"That was for college, Father. The car was—"

"The car was a piece of crap, but he knew how to keep it running, and he didn't learn that from any college. Or anything else useful. What's he doing up there in tree hugger country, for God's sake? Tell you what, until he meets those two conditions and maybe one or two more, he gets nothing. I've written him off."

"Mother can always write him back in after you're gone." Mary smiled to herself as she watched her mother separate eggs and slide the yokes into a bowl of sugar. "That was another joke."

No one was laughing. He'd never be gone. If ever a man was earthbound, it was Dan Tutan. If there was any justice in the world, Mother would outlive him long enough to sell the ranch and blow the proceeds on herself. But Mary had seen enough of the world to know that justice was hard to come by for too many women, and her mother—stirrer of milk, sugar, eggs, anything but controversy—was one of them. She had been living in her husband's pumpkin shell too long.

"We've got the same kind of humor, Daughter. Nobody else gets it."

"Including you and me." Mary folded her arms and watched him walk away. "I wish I could've brought one of the dogs with me," she told her mother quietly. "I miss having one around."

"I wouldn't mind having a dog here again. Would you pour the milk in while I stir?" Mother sidled along the counter to give Mary access to the kettle of scalded milk. "Make sure it's cool enough."

Mary was no judge of cool. She offered the kettle for her mother's parchment-skinned finger test.

Mary nodded, stirred, called for a slow pour and smiled. "Even if you're not doing all the training yourself, Sally's contest might keep you here a little longer than you'd planned."

"I'm here to see you, Mother. The last thing I want to do is cause stress, so…" *So don't spill the milk, Mary. You might end up crying over it.* Her throat stung a little as she swallowed. *Damn hormones.* She took a deep, cleansing breath and set the kettle aside. *Can we talk, Mother? Can we please, just the two of us?* "So you'll tell me if it gets to be too much, won't you? Because obviously nothing's…" *Changed? Wrong choice.* "Nothing's more important right now than your health. Getting you back to a hundred and ten percent."

"Except my hearing." Audrey's eyes brightened with a slow smile. "I like to keep that turned down to about fifty. Every other word is plenty." She nodded toward the refrigerator. "I've already mashed up the strawberries. They're in the—"

"Blue Tupperware box." Mary laughed. She was glad Mother's kitchen hadn't changed.

"The salt is on the front porch, and I have ice in the chest freezer." Audrey folded strawberries into the rich, custardy mixture. "Remember how we used to go out on the porch on summer evenings, and you and the Drexler girls would take turns cranking until you said your arm was going to fall off?" She raised her brow. "You could call them. Tell them we're making ice cream. I'll bet they'd come right over."

"It's just us, Mother. I'll hold the canister, and you pour."

The porch glider squeaked, the ice rattled between the walls of the turquoise bucket and the silver canister, and two meadowlarks called to each other somewhere in the grass. Summer music, Mary told herself as she turned the crank that spun the canister. What had once been a chore now felt like a warm-up for a welcome workout. She'd gone for a run early that morning, but she missed the gym. She wasn't going to give up exercising no matter what. Her face was no prize, but she had a damn good body, and that wasn't going away.

She switched arms. The more resistance, the better the results.

"What the hell is goin' on?"

Stop the music. Here comes Damn Tootin'. He was waving a piece of paper in one hand, an envelope in the other.

"I just got a notice from the Bureau of Land Management, says I can't run cattle in the hills west of Coyote Creek. Says they're designating that area for wildlife. Designating for waste is what that means."

Mary flexed her fingers and stepped back from

the ice cream freezer, which she'd set on a stool. "It's so isolated, Father. Why can't you just let it go?"

"You give 'em an inch, they take a mile. Once they start telling you how to run your business they don't stop."

The glider started squeaking again, albeit tentatively. Audrey's gaze had drifted to the cottonwoods and the Russian olives that formed the windbreak on the north side of the yard. Mary could have followed her mother's lead.

But she didn't.

"Who's *they?*"

"People who don't know what it takes to make a living off this land. They should just stay out of it. Take their damn programs and their so-called *endangered*…" He slapped the envelope against the letter. "There's horses all over this country. Endangered my—" face red, jaw set, he swung his leg up, set the sole of his boot against the edge of the stool and gave a raging shove "—ass!"

Everything flew across the porch—stool, bucket, ice, salt water, canister, pink and white slush.

Mary gaped in horror. "You broke it. Grandma's ice cream—"

"It's not broken," Audrey said, seemingly unruffled. Mary questioned her mother's cool with a look. "I can fix it," Audrey assured her, just as she had the time her father had backed over her tricycle with his little Ford tractor. "Don't worry. I can make more."

"Who the hell is this now?" Dan scowled up the mile-long dirt road that connected the ranch gate with the gravel driveway. A blue pickup pulling a two-horse trailer rumbled in their direction. Three pairs of eyes watched until the vehicle was parked and the driver emerged.

Mary felt a funny little flutter in her chest.

"It's that damn Indian off the Tribal Council. He's the one got them to take my lease land for those mustangs. Dog Track or some damn—"

"Shut up, Dad."

"What?" It was his turn to be horrified. "What did you say to me?"

"You heard me. Do you want to lose the rest of your leases?" She tuned in to the sound of the visitor's footsteps, but she held her father's full attention with a cold glare.

"Looks like somebody spilled her milk."

"It was going to be ice cream." Mentally Mary switched the light off in one room and turned it on in another as Logan mounted the porch steps. "Mother, have you met Logan Wolf Track? Logan, Audrey, my mother. You know my father." Logan glanced at her on the way to shaking her mother's hand, and she reminded him, "You know who he is." With her boots covered in what would have been strawberry ice cream, she didn't feel like saying the name.

But Logan acknowledged him with a proffered

hand. Then he turned to Mary. "Let's go pick up our horse."

"Now?"

"You signed us up. Sally says it's first come, first served. You wanna ride over there with me, or do you have other—"

"What horse?" her father demanded. "You're not bringing any horses here."

"I'm sorry, Logan. My father's a little cranky. He just received some news that didn't sit well with him. We weren't going to bring our horse here, anyway. Were we?"

"Nope." Logan glanced at the mess and gave a perfunctory smile. "Wild horses are real sensitive."

"You mean you're really doing it?" Audrey rose from the glider. "You entered that contest? Are you a horse trainer, Mr. Wolf Track?"

"Among other things," he said.

"Can you give me a minute to clean this up?" Mary moved to pick up the overturned stool, but Logan was closer, and he beat her to it. She got the bucket.

"You go on, Mary. I'll just hose off the porch."

Mary set the bucket on the stool and turned to give the *stay* signal. "You're not hauling hose, Mother."

But Logan was already halfway down the steps. He'd spotted the hose rack, and he was wasting no time. He unlooped the hose, reached over the railing, handed Mary the nozzle and waited for her signal to turn on the water. Her parents watched silently as though they were the visitors. Maybe she and Logan were already a team. Together they made short work of the porch mess.

"Come with us, Mother," Mary offered after Logan turned off the water. She felt like a teenager about to head out on her first date. "We're going to pick out our horse."

"Oh, no." Audrey glanced at Dan, who scowled back at her. She smiled. Actually smiled. "I have so much to do. I'm still going to make ice cream if anyone's interested."

"Damn *right* somebody's interested," Dan grumbled.

"We can do that when I come back. You don't need to be cranking." Mary danced down the porch steps and met Logan at the bottom. "Do you like homemade ice cream?"

"I didn't know it came homemade."

"Give me a ride round trip, and I'll treat you to a taste of heaven." He looked at her as though her head had just turned into a hot fudge sundae. "I'm not kidding," she said. "You'll never go back to the ordinary stuff in a box."

"Haven't even gotten much of that lately." She choked back a laugh as he nodded toward his pickup. "Round trip it is."

She was an interesting woman, all right. Becoming more interesting by the minute. Logan hadn't been around too many women when he was in the army. Just his luck. He could've used a lot more training in that department right about that time in his life. He'd been a skilled hunter and a Golden Gloves champion boxer when he'd enlisted, but he hadn't known jack about women. He'd learned the hard way by getting married and turning in his combat boots without giving either move much thought. He'd been that hungry, and Tonya had been that hot.

So here's this woman offering him ice cream, and his face catches fire. Homemade, she says. What was that supposed to mean?

He was too old to play games. What was that old saying? Burn me once, shame on you. Burn me twice...

He had a history of taking a flirt too seriously.

He'd gone for the hose. He knew what he was doing. Tonya had been older and wiser—well, *smarter*—and she'd been there and gone before he'd known what hit him. A lot of water had flowed under his bridge since then, and he knew how to stay cool. Water was the remedy for hot blood. Sweat, tears, time and the river flowing.

And homemade ice cream was probably just something farmers whipped up when they didn't want to spring for the real thing.

They'd reached the highway, and he was thinking about filling the deafening silence with some country music.

"He never changes."

Her voice startled him. It sounded small—like her mother's, but not worn down. Mary's was more like humiliated. The kid whose father wouldn't quit yelling at the ref. Logan had never actually had a conversation with the man, but Tutan was the kind who made sure everyone knew who he was and acted like they should care. He couldn't get it through his head that non-Indian ranchers didn't call the shots on Indian land. Not anymore. So he'd come before the Council and made a few demands, most recently for reinstatement of the leases he'd lost to the Double D Wild Horse Sanctuary. The Council had given him due consideration—time to tell his side.

He'd leased that land when nobody else wanted it.

Logan would give him that.

He'd been there first.

Logan had laughed out loud.

The Tribe owed him.

Logan had called the question and moved to reaffirm the decision to lease the area known as Coyote Hills to the Drexlers and to honor their nonprofit status with a special rate.

While the voice of a daughter embarrassed by her father's behavior tore at Logan's gut, he couldn't judge another man on that score. He wasn't in the habit of commenting on other people's troubles, anyway, so he said nothing and hoped she'd drop the topic altogether. He was interested in *her*, not her family, even though they had little in common except a horse.

"I worry about my mother."

Even worse. Worrisome mother trumped embarrassing father. And from the look of the three Tutans and the mess on their porch, Mary's worries were well-founded. If it was any of Logan's business, he'd be worried about Mrs. Tutan, too. Fortunately, his interest didn't extend to Mary's mother.

"He's gonna kill her."

Aw, jeez. "Let's go back and get her."

"She won't leave him. I've tried to." His foot on the brake changed her tune. "I don't mean he's going to *kill* her. I mean he's going to be the death of her." She met his glance with an apologetic smile. "I did say *kill*, didn't I."

"You did."

"He doesn't...no. Not literally." She gave a humorless chuckle. "Not *physically.*"

He moved his foot to the accelerator.

"She says she just had a *small* heart attack," Mary said. "What's a small heart attack? She was only in the hospital for two days, but that doesn't mean anything these days. Especially when her husband's big concern is when are they gonna let her out? So that's the only reason I came home. The *main* reason."

Casting about for a cheerful observation, he smiled

at the road ahead. "Now you have a project on the side."

"Good way to keep busy while I'm here."

"Good way to show your father what you're made of."

"I know exactly what I'm made of, and that's all that counts. I've learned that the hard way."

"How many tours?"

"In the Middle East? Two."

He acknowledged her dedication with a raised brow. He'd spent time in the Sandbox, but it had been more than twenty years ago. It had to be tougher these days. It just went on and on, tour after tour for a lot of guys, no end in sight.

A lot of *guys?*

"I don't mind," she was saying. "I love my work."

"What kind of dogs do you train?"

"All kinds. Trackers, sniffers, sentries. Lately I've been coaching Iraqi dog handlers, helping them build their own canine units." She angled her knees in his direction. He'd hit her sweet spot. "I couldn't have a horse when I was growing up, but we had cattle dogs. I learned a lot from them."

That sounded promising. "And you rode Sally's horses."

"As often as I could."

He nodded. "It's been a while since I had a dog. My

sons always had at least one dog around, sometimes one each."

"How many children do you have?" She sounded a little tentative. Disappointed, maybe. She hadn't figured on kids.

"They're not children." *If that helps any.* "Trace and Ethan are in their twenties."

"You don't look old enough to have kids that age. You must've started young."

"As young as I could." He flashed her a wry smile. "I married a family. The boys were half-grown, and I was half-kid. Well, maybe not half, but it was a good mix to start with. We had some good times together." He lifted one shoulder. "We're all on our own now. Full-grown. Divorced. Footloose and...what's the other thing?"

"Fancy free," she quipped, joining him in some irony of her own. "Where is everybody?"

"No idea where their mother is. She cut out early. Left the boys with me."

"What about their father?" She sounded suitably indignant on her new partner's behalf. Logan appreciated loyalty.

It was almost a shame he had to set her straight. Try to, anyway.

"I'm their father. I adopted them, gave them my name. They both go by Wolf Track. Their mother left a picture of her, uh...one of the men. Ethan tried to look him up, but I don't think he got anywhere. The other one..." He glanced at her as he turned onto the gravel approach to the Double D. He'd already said more than he usually did, but the look in her eyes invited more. And, what the hell... "Who knows? She never talked about her past. One of those livin'-in-the-moment people. I liked that about her right up until she was here one moment and gone the next."

"She just...left?"

"Yep. Said she'd come back for the boys and never did."

She didn't look too shocked. Didn't look pitying or superior, wasn't taking him for a saint or a sucker. Maybe she was just taking him for the way he was.

"That must've been hard," she said. "Never know-ing what was going to happen if she came back."

"She wasn't taking those boys, no matter what. Not after..." He smiled as he parked the pickup next to a paddock holding a handful of horses. "You're good at stealing bases, you know that? I never answer questions on the first date."

"This is hardly a date."

"That's right." He cocked his finger and gave her a wink. "I picked you up."

The man winked at her. Winked.

All right, it was kind of cute, but what was he thinking? Mary hadn't been winked at since...never?

She didn't remember anybody winking at her. It made her feel downright giddy. Of course, she'd hidden it.

Well, except for a little smile.

Hoolie Hoolihan emerged from the bunkhouse and ambled across the graveled quad that was surrounded by outbuildings and corrals. Hoolie was a true cowboy—unchanging, ageless, loyal as an old soldier. As far as Mary knew, he'd always been part of Double D. He greeted her with a proper pull on the brim of his cowboy hat before shaking Logan's hand, tucking thumbs in his belt and commenting on the need for some rain. The visitors chimed in as they drifted toward the corral. As though they'd been cued, the horses suddenly took to the far corner like a flight of butterflies.

"Sally's pretty pleased with herself, gettin' you two partnered up," Hoolie said as he hiked one boot up to the bottom fence rail. "Which one are you taking?"

"We're going with Mary's first instinct. Taking the claybank." Logan glanced at his partner. "Right?"

"He's beautiful," Mary said, basking in his approval.

"That one's all mustang," Hoolie said. "No plow-horse blood in those legs."

Logan smiled. "That's the way we like 'em." At the moment, he only had eyes for the horses.

"I've got your book," Hoolie said.

Logan spared him an appreciative grin. "So *you're* the one."

"The Indian way of training horses takes a lotta time, seems like."

"I've been doing it all my life," Logan quipped.

"You think you can have the horse ready in just—"

"Oh, yeah." Logan smiled, still watching the horses. "I don't know if I can have Sergeant Tutan ready, but the horse is not a problem."

"Are you taking him to your place?" Mary asked.

"First thing, I'm taking him back to his place. You can come if you want. Otherwise I can drop you off."

"*His* place?"

"He's a wild horse. His place is wild. That's where we start." Logan turned to Hoolie. "Can you help me cut him out?"

"I'll be the gate man."

Hoolie headed for the barn. Mary followed Logan around the front of his pickup to the empty horse trailer.

"*Where* are we starting?" she asked as she watched him open the tack door and reach inside for a coiled hard-twist rope. "*I'm going,* but I'm just curious."

"His place." He slid the bolt on the tack door and slid Mary a playful smile. "You like camping?"

She laughed. "I'm a soldier. Camp is *my* place."

Chapter Three

He had set up his camp the day Mary had signed the agreement. The tipi was traditional. Except for its shape, the round pen was not. He had a permanent one in his backyard, but he used portable corral panels to make the circle he required in pursuit of his acquaintance with a horse. The round pen served as physical containment, but it allowed for freedom of the spirit. The rope he had watched many a tamer use to "break" a horse generally served Logan as a director's tool. It helped him extend his arm or widen his hand. He could've used something else, but he was still a cowboy, and the rope was part of his gear.

And he was still an Indian. Gone were the old government-issue canvas tents his grandfather's generation had known all too well. "Back to the blanket" had been an expression of ridicule. Back to the tipi was a summertime homecoming. Sure, he lived in a house. Most days, anyway. But there was no better shelter for camping at a powwow or getting away to a place where there were no square corners and no one knew your name than a Lakota tipi.

He'd set it up in a grassy draw in a remote part of the sanctuary. There was a stand of scrub oaks with a plentiful supply of deadfall, a patch of buffalo berry bushes, shifting shade, a view of mighty South Dakota buttes, and a sun-catcher creek meandering through it all.

He could feel Mary's pleasure at first sight. She drew a quick breath and took it in wordlessly, which pleased him. Her curiosity was fully satisfied, and no comment could improve on that.

He backed the trailer up to the round pen, and she helped him adjust the panels to create a funnel into the circle from the trailer door. Logan entered the trailer through the front door, and the mustang scrambled out the back and darted to the far side of the pen. Logan half expected the horse to jump the fence. He could have cleared it, and Logan would have had all kinds of hell to pay getting him back. The fact that he didn't try told Logan something about his state of mind. He wasn't as scared as he looked.

Logan signaled Mary to stay where she was, partly

hidden by the trailer door. Give everybody's pulse rate a chance to settle down. His own sure was racing. This was the all-things-being-equal time. None of them knew the roles of the other two. If they were to spend time together—any time worth spending— they would find comfortable ways to fit with each other. But right now they were three individuals, each looking out for number one.

The gelding paced nervously, but his ears were working the space. Logan would let him have all the time he needed. He was already impressed with his partner's ability to read his cues. When the mustang settled down, dropped his head and sniffed the grass he'd trampled all but flat, Logan moved in and started easing the fence panels, closing off the circle. Mary followed his lead without discussion.

Mary knew better than to chat up a trainer when he was working. She hated nothing more than another human voice confusing the animal and impeding her progress. She was probably boring to watch. But Logan was not. He wasn't doing much, wasn't saying anything, but every move he made was fascinating. He was long and lanky, and he moved so smoothly it was hard to tell how quick he was. Every aspect of his attention focused on the animal, intent on nonverbal means of show and tell. His hands were sure, his arms powerful, his back long and tapered, his face enormously attractive. Granted, some of that had no effect on the horse, but it surely sucked her in.

Once initial acquaintances had been made, Logan filled a hay net with alfalfa from his pickup and pushed a small galvanized steel water trough halfway under the fence. Mary went after the five gallon rubber water bucket she'd noticed in the trailer's storage compartment and headed for the creek, smiling at him in passing. "Thought I'd fetch a pail of water." He started to follow, but it was her turn to give the signal to stay. "I've got it under control, Jack." She glanced up at his hat. "Watch out for your crown."

"Don't take any tumbles without me."

"You're thinking of Jill. I'm Mary. The contrary sister."

"You feel like roasting a few dogs over a fire, Mary? That's all I've got." He grinned. "Unless you brought your little lamb."

"You're heartless," she said as she sashayed down the slope, swinging her bucket.

"Yeah, I gave that away a long time ago," he called after her. "Got myself a mechanical ticker. No more tears."

"Right. The truth is, I've been in the army long enough, I'll eat almost anything. Just don't tell me what it is."

He offered to help her carry the water up the hill, but she noticed he didn't push when she said she had it. When she told him she was going back down to the creek for some dried wood she'd spotted, he grinned and called her his kind of woman. She figured there was a dig in there somewhere, but his smile was so infectious she didn't care. His dark eyes glittered with unqualified delight.

They had fun with their fire making, traded hot dog jokes, enjoyed the fry bread his sister had given him that morning in return for snaking out a clogged drain. They traded smiles when they heard their mustang take a drink from the trough. Twilight settled in softly. Crickets sang to each other in the tall grass. Mary happily inhaled the smell of horse sweat from the blanket Logan had provided her to sit on. She figured being covered with horse hair would be a lateral move from being covered with dog hair. Hair came with the territory.

But the view was novel, and what Mary was viewing right now was an Indian cowboy stretched out long, lean and relaxed, elbow braced on the ground, sipping black coffee from a blue metal cup. She'd been around a lot of men in her line of work, but Logan was different. Maybe the difference was mostly in her head, but the view was definitely stirring.

"Whose land is this now? Sally's or my father's?" Logan gave her a hooded look, and she took it to mean that she ought to have known. "I never came out this far when I was living here."

"Never?"

She shook her head slowly. She would not tell him

how, once she'd signed her enlistment papers, she'd started counting the days until she would finally see what South Dakota looked like from the air. This was a beautiful place—the mustang's place, Logan's and Sally's, and, yes, her father's—but Mary had never been anywhere else before she'd taken that flight to Fort Leonard Wood, the first of many flights and many new sights. Granted, few were this beautiful, but she'd welcomed every takeoff knowing that she'd learned more about the world at every landing.

"This is Indian land," Logan said. "It doesn't matter who's using it."

"I'm not sure what my father would use it for. Hunting, maybe." Her father had never been much of a hunter himself, but he'd made friends with influential people by hosting hunting parties. She hoped they hadn't partied here. "This must be where the wild things are."

"Some," Logan allowed. "Not enough, if you ask me. We could do with more wild things."

"Instead, we're about to *un*do." Mary glanced toward their mustang. "This one, anyway."

"This is the one you picked. You signed and sealed his fate."

"And it's up to you to see that *we* deliver. As we say in the army, the fate of the many depends on a few."

"Hear that, boy?" Logan called over his shoulder. "It's for your brothers and sisters."

"You do believe that, don't you? It's a good cause."

"Of course I believe it. It's what I do." He sat up slowly, flexing his shoulders within the confines of what she judged to be a fairly new, crisp denim jacket. "Two animals came to live among the Lakota—the horse and the dog. It's an agreement those animals were willing to make. Not all of them, but a few."

"What if this one doesn't agree?"

"Then we agree to let him go, and we ask someone else. Isn't that what you do? Not all dogs agree to your training."

"No, but I can identify the disagreeable ones almost immediately." She smiled. "It's what I do, Mr. Wolf Track."

"Where do the disagreeable ones go?"

"Back where they came from."

"The wild?" He shook his head. "No. With dogs, you either have to care for them or put them down. Even the wild ones—the wolves and the coyotes— they're barely tolerated."

"A wild dog isn't the same as a wolf or coyote."

"True. In some ways a feral dog has more in common with a feral horse."

"Except in the eyes of the law."

He nodded toward the round pen. "This guy's lucky. If he can't live tame, he can still live free. For now, at least, thanks to the law and the Double

D Wild Horse Sanctuary. Both subject to the whims of politics."

"Now that the Tribal Council has stepped in on behalf of the sanctuary..."

"Tribal politics is still politics," he allowed with a shrug. "But your instincts are good, and you chose well."

"With a little guidance," she allowed back. "How long will you stay out here?"

"Until he agrees to live among people."

"That sounds pretty mystical."

"Good. That's what I'm goin' for." He looked up, a new sparkle in his eyes. "Psychology is out. It's mysticism that sells these days."

"That's right. You wrote a book. I'd better get a copy so I can start doing some homework."

"Wait for the next edition." He grinned. "First one's out of print."

"They'll print more, won't they?"

"Yeah, if I revise it—put a hook into it, like whispering or shape-shifting, something like that. I just wrote about gentling horses. I didn't get into any mysticism. I figured, you write about talking to animals, you got yourself a kids' book."

She laughed. "So you're working on a revised edition."

"Thinkin' about it. I don't wanna come off sounding like some Hollywood Indian."

"But you're not one. Whatever you say is going to sound like a South Dakota Indian."

"That's not what you want to hear."

"Me?"

"You in general. *People.*" He leaned closer with that engaging glint in his eyes. "I thought you'd like the idea of making an agreement with the animal, but you didn't really buy in."

"Yes, I did," she said too quickly. "I totally bought in."

"No, you didn't. You said it *sounded* mystical. You nibbled at the bait, but you didn't swallow my hook."

"Maybe I don't need a hook. I'm not *people in general.* I'm a trainer. I'm already interested. But for the general population, why not use your profile on the cover?" She took his chin in hand and turned his head to the side. "Now there's a hook."

He laughed, and then he turned his head slowly, his chin still resting in her hand. Their eyes met on a willingness to exchange something more.

Lean closer.

You first.

He smiled. *Not yet.*

She withdrew her hand and glanced away. The tingling in her hand had spread to every nerve in her body. A disconcerting moment of the kind best left to eighth graders.

She cleared her throat. "You wouldn't have an extra vehicle, would you?"

"You mean one that runs?"

"I'll ask Sally. You can just drop me off at the Double D."

"Drop you off? I thought we were in this together."

"We are." *And I thought you were going to kiss me.* "But I can't *stay* here. I didn't bring any stuff."

"What do you need?"

"Not much, but I thought this was just a go-see. I wasn't planning on staying."

"I don't know what it's like in today's army, but my tipi is a step up from what barracks life was like in my day." He tipped his head to one side and surveyed the structure from the ground up. The tips of more that a dozen pine lodge poles pointed toward a smattering of early stars in the purpling sky. "Decorated it myself," he said of the canvas skin.

Mary recognized a howling gray wolf on one side of the door and his tracks leading around the circle and out of sight. On the other side of the door a paint horse seemed to be racing for shelter, leaving tracks of his own. She wondered what happened behind the tent.

"You were in the army?"

"Gulf War. Show me an Indian man hasn't served some time in the military, I'll show you one…" He glanced skyward and sighed. "...probably did time somewhere else."

"What about women?"

"Some. Not as many. It's more like a man thing."

"Really."

He smiled. "Really."

Drop it, Mary. Back away quietly.

Not a chance.

"You wouldn't want your daughter to be a soldier?"

"Never thought about it." He sipped his coffee— which must have been cold by now—pressed his full lips together, apparently mulling it over now that she'd mentioned it. "If I had a daughter, I guess it would be up to her. You want to protect your women and children, seems like."

"Protect, or control?"

"My older son never enlisted. The younger one...." He lifted one shoulder. "Didn't suit him. He went AWOL and got himself booted out."

"Where are they?"

"Not too sure," he said dismissively as he nodded toward her plate and the canned pork and beans she hadn't touched. "Sorry about the meal. I'm not much of a cook."

"No, it's fine." She reached out, tipped her plate sideways over the fire and let the beans slide off and sizzle in the low flame. "It's just that my mother hasn't given me a chance to get hungry. I've been trying to get her to rest, but whenever I turn my back on her, she sneaks into the kitchen and starts rattling those pots and pans."

"I like that tune. It's been a while since I heard it."

"Me, too."

"Whatever's handy."

"I know what you mean. And I'll get the next round." She set the blue enamelware plate aside. "It's not about eating or sleeping here—I'd be fine here— it's about my mother. I really should…" *Tell the truth, Mary.* "I'd much rather be here. I'm such a selfish person. I came to be with her for…" *The partial truth and nothing but the-tip-of-the-iceberg truth.* "Well, for a little while. Ignore everything else and give her the kind of attention she never…"

She sighed and shook her head, exactly the way he had done a moment ago. He had his stuff, too. Stuff he clearly didn't want popping out all over the place, which said a lot about him. No doubt in her mind he'd been a good soldier, which was something she still aspired to be, all scrubbed and polished, crisply pressed and neatly buttoned up.

"But I can't stay there twenty-four seven," she said. "I'll go crazy. I'll say things, and I'll…" She glanced toward the round pen. Their mustang stood quietly, his pale ears cocked in their direction as though their conversation mattered to him, too. Mary smiled.

"This is good. This will really be good. I'm excited about it, and I know she understands. I'll be able to stay out of his way if I'm involved in something else. Else*where.*"

"That's good, because I want to start our boy in his territory. No distractions except us. Between us, one or the other should be here." She turned to him, and he nodded. "Twenty-four seven, just about."

"That sounds like the makings of a schedule."

"I have a meeting tomorrow afternoon."

"I could be here early if I had a way to get here," she said cheerfully. "I'm good with schedules."

"That makes one of us."

Logan didn't mind picking her up, but there seemed to be no shortage of vehicles at the Tutan place—a brand new shortbox pickup sitting in the driveway and an older three-quarter ton backed up to a side door down at the barn—and he wondered why she couldn't use one of them while she was home. He parked his pickup, knocked on the front door, and remembered the reason.

"I'm here for Mary," Logan said through the screen in the top of the storm door.

"She's expecting you." Tutan called his daughter's name as though he had her warming the far end of the bench, and then he stepped onto the porch, hand on the door handle, shoulder propping it open. He could easily suck back into his lair if Logan tried anything funny, right? Like handing him a religious tract or a catalog for cleaning products. "That's the big line now, isn't it?" Tutan said with a smile. "*I'm here for you.* I hear they love that." He did another one-eighty toward the deep shadows. "Mary! Your new boyfriend's here."

"Her ride," Logan amended, keeping a firm grip on his cool.

"She's busy upstairs with her mother, but if you want, you can wait in the kitchen. There's coffee. Hope you don't mind, but I've got work to do."

"I'll wait out here."

"Hell, no. That ice cream mess is still drawing flies out here."

Logan stepped into the foyer, but that was as far as he was going. No parlor, thank you very much.

"Mary!" Tutan tucked his thumbs under his drooping paunch and into his belt. "She comes home and says *I'm here for you, Mother.* Next thing you know it's *Can I borrow the pickup?* And the answer is *Hell, no, you can't take the pickup.* Some things never change, and that conversation seems to be one of them." Over the shoulder and into the pine panel-lined darkness. "Mary!"

Mary appeared with a loaded laundry basket, peered past her father and greeted Logan with a smile.

"Morning," he said heartily, and she responded in kind.

"What's going on back there?" Tutan demanded. "Is she sick again?"

"She's cleaning again. I caught her taking curtains down in the bedrooms."

Audrey emerged from the same darkness. "Nobody's been using the children's rooms much, and everything's just so dusty."

"I'll be right with you," Mary called out, and then lowered her voice. "I'll take this stuff down to the laundry room, and you can wash to your heart's content, Mother, but please wait for me to put the curtains back up."

"You'll be back, then."

"I'll be back."

"No hurry," Audrey said as Mary disappeared through another door. "I'm just glad you'll be here awhile longer." She took two tentative steps toward Logan. "I think it's exciting, you two working as a team."

"Yes, ma'am," Logan quipped with a wink for the older woman. Her blue eyes brightened, and her powder-pale face colored up some. Logan wished he'd brought her something more. Something sweet that she didn't have to make herself. Awkward as hell, her husband standing there like he might pounce if Logan overstepped some invisible boundary.

"Mary says you wrote a horse training book," Audrey said. "I'm trying to get her to write about training dogs. You should see what her dogs can—"

"I'll be back at noon," Tutan told his wife. "I'll have some of that German potato salad you were talking about. And make some bratwurst with it." He spared Mary some kind of a warning glance as she made another entrance. "If it's not too much for you to handle."

"It's in the refrigerator. All she has to do is heat it up," Mary said. "Remember what I said, Mother. If you need me, call Sally. She knows where to find me."

Man, it was a relief to get out of that house. Logan gunned his pickup engine and headed for the Tutan gate like a barn-sour horse. Mary was quiet, probably just as relieved as he was. He smiled to himself as he thought about the council meeting and his motion to lease land to the Drexlers instead of Dan Tutan. *Good move, Track Man.*

She was staring out the window. He couldn't see much of her face, but he could feel her emptiness. "Thought you didn't know how to cook," he said.

"I said I'm not much of a cook." She turned to him, eyes hard, smile tight. "But I sure know how to take instruction."

"Good. I'm looking for ways to improve on mine, so maybe you can give me some pointers. Ways people can understand as easily as horses."

"My people?"

"Your people, my people, *most* people. Your mom's right—you've had some valuable experience. It's one thing to be able to train animals, but teaching people to train animals—teaching people to do *anything*—hell, that takes some serious patience. And you're working with people who live in a whole different world." He flashed an encouraging smile. "You've gotta be gifted."

"The dogs are gifted. All I do is put their gifts to use."

"I like that," he enthused. "Can I use it?"

"Be my guest. But I want credit." She was smiling now. "Better yet, cash."

"No hands," Logan admonished as Mary extended hers in some sort of a cautionary signal. He'd told her not to let the horse come off the fence. "Not yet. He doesn't trust hands. His kind doesn't have them."

"You said to bring my skills to—"

"Not yet. Think about the dogs. How do they feel about your hands?"

"I teach them to respond to hand signals."

"Down the road. We're starting off in the horse's world. No hands today."

Logan took great pleasure in watching Mary become acquainted with the mustang. Most people wanted to rush the ground work. *How long before we get to ride him?* Both his boys had been impatient, but especially Trace, who'd found his niche bucking them out in the rodeo arena. Ethan had surprised him. For all his younger son's defiance, he'd eventually taken Logan's way to heart. He'd seen first hand what the boy could do under some pretty humbling circumstances. He imagined introducing Mary to his boys, but in his mind's eye the boys were kids. Mary was...

Fearless. The woman knew her way around animals. She didn't push, but neither did she back away. She had the mustang running circles around her, wearing himself down of his own accord, discovering that he was safe with her. He might even be able to trust her. She was the kind of person a team captain picked first. If she didn't know how to play, she'd soon learn and she'd be there come rain or shine. No-nonsense Mary. She wore a T-shirt and jeans, and her hair was clipped back in a cute ponytail. He wondered why she wasn't wearing a hat. She was a soldier, after all.

"You ready to take a break?"

Mary looked at him as though he were talking nonsense. He grinned because he knew just how she felt. *A break from what? Hanging out with a friend?* It was hardly a strain, and you hated to walk away when you could feel a connection in the making.

He waved a bottle of water, and her face brightened. "Oh, yeah." She checked the horse's trough for water on her way to joining Logan. They sat in the grass a couple of feet from the pen and watched the mustang while they drank. Logan nodded when the horse took their cue. He moved to the trough and had himself a good long drink. Good sign. When the time came, Logan would not want to give this guy up. But the project had a greater purpose.

"Sally has the right idea," he said. "Persuade the two-leggeds to save some room for the four-leggeds by making more of them *useful*."

"Us or them?" Mary rolled the plastic bottle back and forth across her brow. "Who's making who useful?"

"Whom," he teased as he took off his straw hat and put it on her head. "Better watch your language around me, Sergeant."

"Whom, then. I have absolutely no illusion about who's making *whom* useful in the case of my job. My nose is worthless. My bark is way worse than my bite. Being in charge is highly overrated."

He laughed. "You won't have to worry about that for a while. You're not wearing any stripes."

"How many did you have?" He questioned her with a look. "When you got out, how many stripes?"

"I left their uniform on the table, collected my honorable discharge along with my pay and moved on."

"Were you married then?"

He took a long pull from the water bottle. "Technically, but not for long, as it turned out. She'd already gotten a head start with the movin' on part."

"And left you with her children?"

"You know, you've got a pretty nose. But you're

right—it's not your best feature." He lifted the brim of his hat to her hairline and smiled. "That would be your eyes. They're like glass. Feel like I'm peekin' in your windows." He gave her earlobe a playful tug. "But you've gotta use these if you want this thing to work."

"What thing?"

"This thing we've started." He nodded toward the mustang, who was sniffing the grass in the center of the pen. "Nose, eyes, ears, hands—bring all that into that pen right there, that circle. And your gut."

"My gut," she echoed dubiously.

"Right here." He moved his hand from her ear to her abdomen—skipping over the interesting parts in between—and pressed lightly. "You know what I'm talking about from your dogs. But in your relationship with a horse, this is even more important. Almost as important as it is with a man."

She looked surprised, but she didn't flinch. His gaze held hers. Or maybe it was the other way around. It didn't matter. The message was unmistakable. Neither of them had been looking for it, but here it was. Inescapable mouth-to-mouth magnetism. They had two free arms between them. His slid around her back, hers around his neck. He started slowly—a tentative taste, a tender tease, delicious anticipation.

He bumped into his hat, nudged it back and touched his forehead to hers. "I have to go."

"Of course you do." She swept his hat off her head and put it on his.

"Committee meeting," he explained. "I won't be gone long. Will you be okay here for a while?"

"Should I do more ground work?"

"All you need to do is be there with him. Pay attention. I want to know what you learn from him. I'll be back in a couple of hours, and I'll bring supper. Meanwhile..." He put his hat back on her and tapped the crown for emphasis. "Wear this."

She had no idea how much time had passed when the peace was shattered by the noise of an approaching vehicle. A little irritating at first, but the sight of Hank Night Horse giving Sally a hand in getting down from his lofty pickup cab made Mary smile. They made an even prettier sight swishing through the buffalo grass arm in arm and peering over the fence. Love was in the air.

Mary met them at the fence. "I think we're becoming friends, too."

"I knew you would." Sally glanced pointedly at Logan's hat. "Looks good on you."

"I mean the horse and I." Mary turned to admire the mustang, who stood calmly at the far side of the pen. "My assignment was to pay attention the whole afternoon, but he's way ahead of me. His attention is far more focused than mine." She turned back to the visitors. "Did my mother call you?"

"No, but your friend did. Said you were out here alone."

"He had to go to a meeting." And he was thinking about her, which was nice. But the blue pickup barreling toward them wasn't his. "Who's this?"

"Annie. We're lending you some wheels."

"Oh, no, that's not—"

"It is. I don't know how long Logan intends to stay out here—nobody seems to know exactly how he does what he does…" Sally looked up at Hank. "Do they?"

"Don't look at me. Just because we're all related doesn't mean we all know each other."

"Or each other's secrets?"

"Secrets, yeah. We all know the secrets." Hank laid a hand on Sally's slight shoulder. "And you're not gettin' 'em, woman. Everything else I have is yours, but not the code. I'd be drummed out of Indian Country."

"Logan is Hank's sister-in-law's cousin," Sally told Mary.

"Uncle," Hank amended. He smiled. "Like you say, it's all relative."

"When did I say that? Relative, related, relations…" Sally laughed. "Since I started hanging out with this man, I've begun to rethink the *R* word."

"I did that a long time ago." Mary glanced at the vehicle Ann was parking behind the monster truck Hank had driven. "I'll admit, it would make things easier, but are you sure you want to leave your pickup with me, Annie?"

"Oh, no, I can't leave Zelda Blue. She belongs to my husband."

"My husband." Sally leaned close to Mary. "She sure likes the taste of those words. Sweet enough to turn her cheeks pink."

Ann licked her lips, eyes dancing.

"So we're leaving you the Double D dually," Sally said. "Don't let anybody deface the new logo." She reached through the fence and touched Mary's arm. "Just kidding."

Mary nodded, but she felt the spirit draining from her smile. Her father's bitterness was no joke, and they both knew it. She stole a glance at Hank Night Horse, who eyed her right back. A warning, maybe. Whether she'd asked for it or not, Sally had a protector now, and as long as Mary had a foot in each opposing camp Hank didn't trust her. The look he gave her said it all.

"Oh, look," Mary said, turning all eyes to the horizon. "Logan's back already."

She climbed over the fence and dropped to the ground like an eager recruit.

Chapter Four

"I cut the meeting short," Logan announced as he emerged from his pickup, brown paper bag in hand. "Looks like I just made it for this one."

"It's almost over. We brought your partner a set of wheels, but we don't want to get in the way of the program," Sally said. "It's good you've got her workin' it."

"Come have some coffee. You guys hungry?" Logan nodded toward Mary. "This one doesn't cook, so I picked up some ready-to-eat."

"This one?" Mary glanced at the other two women. "As opposed to that one and the other one?"

"The other one would like to get back home," Ann said. "To her husband."

"Excuse my sister's manners. The honeymoon continues." Sally turned to Logan. "So, tell us about this code you guys have."

"What code?"

"This is what brings men to their knees every time. They sound so innocent, and they smell so sweet." Hank put his arm around Sally's shoulders and pitched his voice up an octave. "Give us the code, boys. You can trust us."

"The *secret* code," Sally prodded.

"The one we use on the Moccasin Telegraph," Hank added.

"Oh, *that* code." Logan shook his head. "Sorry, ladies. That's sacred."

Hank nodded. "You got your Morse code. We've got our MT code."

"Emp-ty?" Mary chuckled.

"That's all you'll get out of me," Hank said. "That's what we call it. We figure it's safe as long as you think there's nothing in it."

Sally leaned back for a look past Hank's shoulder. "Annie, where are you going?"

"Personally, I wouldn't mind staying to watch the girls talk the boys out of their decoder rings, but Zelda's got work to do." She tossed her keys up and caught them. "And these people have cold burgers to choke down."

"My day's not over either," Hank said. He tapped Logan's shoulder with his fist. "Hang in there, man."

"Well, damn," Sally said. "I guess that means we're leaving. Unfortunately I have some calls to make. We're looking for twenty-five competitors, and we're still ten short."

"You're too picky," Hank said.

"Selective." Sally nodded toward the tipi. "I'm bringing the camera next time I come out. This is perfect for the calendar."

Ann stopped in her tracks. *"What* calendar?"

"The wild horse calendar." Sally grinned. "Part promotion, part fundraiser. I was going to do trainer of the month, but the applicants aren't falling into the two cake flavors I was hoping for—cheese and beef—so I'm looking for Western romance."

The men exchanged glances.

"Humor me," Sally said. "It's for a good cause."

"I can come back and get you guys later," Ann suggested. "Cake is not on my diet."

"C'mon, woman. I'll humor you." Hank squeezed Sally's shoulders. "You want something to pin on your wall?"

"It won't be cold beef," Logan said as they stood together watching the couple walk away, the man steadying the woman while the woman lifted the man.

So that's what a good fit looks like, Mary thought. Separately they looked like pieces from two totally different toys, like Lincoln Logs and an Erector Set. It must have taken some serious creativity—not to mention courage—to put one and one together. *This one and that one*. Neither part was pushing to reshape the other, but they were moving in sync. Amazing.

If anyone could do the math, of course, Sally could. No matter what kind of division had been done on her, Sally could rebuild from the smallest remainder. Small but mighty, that was Sally. Mary didn't have that kind of imagination. She preferred to do her thinking inside the box. Much safer. Sure, she'd traveled a lot, but she'd taken the box with her. She was a turtle and her best friend was a hare, but there was no contest. Venturing outside the box was a stupid move for a turtle.

But, oh, that hare truly made it look tempting.

"Is that what we're having?" She reached for Logan's paper bag. "Ready to eat last Thursday?"

He swung the bag out of reach. "You think you can do better?" She lunged for the bag. He dodged easily. "Show me what you got."

"I got a promise from you." She grabbed for the bag again, and he laughed. "Supper, you said."

"And you can have it the way it is, or you can heat it up. What you can't do is pin it to your wall."

"I don't have a wall."

"No trophy room?" He dropped the bag, and she caught it. "Quick hands," he said with a smile. He snatched at his hat, which she instinctively tried to defend. "But not quick enough."

"If I had a trophy room, I'd be selective in what I'd display. Who says you'd make the cut?"

"Nice steal. You've played this—"

She grabbed the cowboy hat back and hoisted it overhead, grinning. "*That's* a steal."

"We've got two different games going here."

She whipped hat and bag behind her back. "And I have both balls."

"Ouch."

"That's right." She tucked her bottom lip between her teeth and challenged him with a come-on look. "I do the cutting and the pinning." She dodged his reach. "And the sewing. Which means I get to wear the—"

He faked left, trapped right and hauled her against him with her arms locked firmly behind her back, her wrists manacled. "Pants?" he taunted. "Who says I'd want your pants?"

"I…"

He dipped his head. She lifted her chin, expecting a kiss but he faked her out again. He slid his smooth cheek against hers and nuzzled her ear while he shifted his thighs and pressed her tighter to him. "They wouldn't fit me, would they," he said softly.

"No."

"No, what?"

"You're too big for my britches."

"Mm-hmm." He nipped her earlobe. "I'll wear mine. You wear yours." He scooped the lobe into his mouth with his tongue and sucked noisily. "Mmm, this *is* better. A little salty, but that's the way I like them."

"I still have...both..."

"I know." He moved his head up and down slowly, abrading her cheek as he kept the pressure between them steady. She moved her hips, mimicking his movements. "Mmm, yeah, this is the way this game is played. Your court. My..." He turned his lips to her temple. "If we don't take a time out, I'm gonna score."

"You think so, huh?"

"Slam dunk or kiss off the glass?" He leaned back smiling. "What's your pleasure?"

"Not telling." She wasn't smiling. "Not on my court. You have to work for it."

"Of course I do." He claimed his property back— actually, she let the hat and the bag slide, and he caught them—and stepped back. He winked at her. "Wouldn't have it any other way. Ready to eat?"

"Bring it on," she said. He put his hat on, opened the bag, and she took a look. Fry bread on top of Styrofoam boxes. "Where's the beef?"

"You wanna start with the main course?" He took a peek, sniffed, closed the bag and shrugged. "It's what's for dinner." He looked at her thoughtfully. "You're not hungry, are you?"

She shook her head. He held her gaze for a long moment, telling her it was her move. She glanced up at his hat. "That belongs on you. I'll bring a cap next time."

"You're on leave." He put the cowboy hat back on her, adjusted the brim. "Looks good on you." He grinned. "You've got a big head."

"The better to outthink you with, Mr. Wolf Track."

"So, tell me, what have you learned about this boy?" He laid a hand on her back and guided her toward the round pen, setting dinner aside on the hood of his pickup as he passed. "Has he told you his name?"

"No, not yet. But I told him mine. I told him..." She rested her forearms on the top rail. The mustang eyed her from the far side of the circle. "I don't like keeping him in this pen."

"Maybe we should let him go."

"No, that's not what I was thinking when I said that. I was thinking that this is the hard part for both of us. We're strangers. I'm the only thing standing between him and his freedom."

"It's the pen." Logan gripped the rail and gave it a little shake. "If it was just you, he'd be long gone."

"It feels different with a wild animal. It almost feels..."

"You're taking it too personal. He's been penned up before." He turned his back to the fence and leaned against it. "Anyway, I'm the one who put him in there."

"He's not really scared anymore, but he doesn't feel safe, either. He's watching. Waiting." He wasn't the only one. She couldn't look the mustang in the eye, but she didn't have to. She felt it intensely. "Wanting."

"He needs a family. We're going to fill that role."

"You mean a herd." She packed down the feelings and turned to Logan with the cerebral stuff. Facts. "Like a dog needs a pack. We become the alpha, the—"

"Family," he insisted. "First we convince him we're not gonna eat him, and we don't do that by thinking like dogs."

"I realize a herd is different from a pack—horses are prey and dogs are predators—but there's still a pecking order."

"Totally different worlds. You know what the beauty of being human is? We can be anything we want to be if we put our minds to it."

"Doctor, tailor, soldier, sailor?" She smiled.

"Two-legged, four-legged, winged or finned. You can put yourself in any kind of skin, imagine yourself there." He glanced from her eyes to his hat, as though her head might be doing something in there besides taking cover. "If you put your mind to it."

"I can do that." Imagining herself somewhere else *was* her cover.

"It shows. And that's why we're in this to-gether."

He sent her back into the round pen to repeat many of the actions and much of the inaction she'd applied previously. She could feel the mustang coming to her in some strange way. Logan was right about the point of contact. It was gut level, and it was unsettling. But it was real, and it was different from any communication she'd experienced. She wanted to call it something so she could put it in its place. File it in a box so she could use it effectively. Safely. She loved her dogs for accepting her unconditionally, but this gut-level connection with the horse was a little intimidating. She really wanted him to like her. Trust her. He was honest and pure, and his acceptance suddenly felt all-important.

Which was probably crazy, but it was as good a test as any for a directionally impaired person sitting at a crossroads without a map.

She knew the way back to her mother's house, but she would have a little campfire time first. Without asking, Mary gathered wood and filled the fire pit. Without discussion, Logan brought out the blankets, lit the kindling, and tossed a handful of sage into the mix. Bit by bit the small, curling leaves became pungent white smoke. The soft summer wind had settled, and a distant butte had sucked the sun into its pocket, but there was plenty of light and no shortage of background music from the tiny musicians in the grass.

Mary took her time with her food. She wanted to eat enough to show her appreciation but not so much that the show backfired on her. The fried food required delicate handling. Little bites, lots of chews. If he noticed, he didn't show it. She closed the Styrofoam lid on half eaten chicken and fry bread, avoiding his eyes as she thanked him and said it was good.

He chuckled.

"No, really. I'll do the dishes and take the trash out."

"You're a good camper."

"And a happy one," she said cheerfully as she stuffed the paper bag.

"Too bad we didn't bring a dog along."

"I don't feed mine scraps. They eat better than I do."

"We'll do beef next time, I promise."

"Oh, no, this was fine. You know what it's like when you go home to Mother. She's not happy unless you're eating." She sat cross-legged, hands braced on her knees. "You know how it is when you're out in the field. Your stomach shrinks."

"You like your job?"

"I do. Very much."

He poked at the flaming firewood with a stick.

"I was in the Air Cav. Funny, huh? An Indian in the cavalry?"

"Not these days. Did you like your job?"

"Some days. I was a kid. I loved those big choppers." His eyes brightened. "Rappelling! Didn't get to rap jump often enough, but when I did, man…" He shook his head, smiling as his stick sent up a shower of sparks. "That was always a good day. As long as you weren't getting shot at. Not *that* big of an adrenaline junkie."

Yeah, right. The Screaming Eagles pissed pure adrenaline.

"I wanted to get away. That's why I enlisted." Mary smiled sweetly. "I've traveled, learned so much, met people. It's been a good life."

"Has been? Sounds like you're thinking of making some changes."

"I really do like my job. I think I could do it as a civilian. You know, train…" She was straying into speculative territory. Uncharted waters, poor visibility. "What about you? You have two jobs and two sons. A full life."

"Mmm-hmm." He eyed her for a moment. "What do you wanna know?"

"Do your sons live around here? What do they do?" She smiled. "Are you a grandfather?"

"My sons have no children." He lifted one shoulder. "As far as I know."

"They aren't close by?"

"Trace—the older one—he's a professional rodeo cowboy. I see him once in a while. He's out in Wyoming. And Ethan…" He stared into the fire. "Ethan's been working with horses, too."

"Both following in their dad's footsteps."

"I wouldn't say that. Each one is doin' his own thing in his own way."

"Where's Ethan?"

"Last I heard he was in Colorado. It's been a while since I saw him. He keeps in touch with Trace."

"So you know he's safe and healthy."

"If he's not, he knows where to find me." He tossed the stick into the flames. "Never turn your back on family. Those ties are thicker than blood. You get 'em all twisted up, you can choke on 'em."

"I'm not the one who's twisted," she said quietly.

"Then you'll be okay." A sudden breeze sent wood smoke into his face. He slid closer to her, turning a coughing jag into a laugh. "Hey, you feel like you're choking, step back. Catch your breath. Come out here and…" He coughed again. "…and be with your horse. This is why the man sits opposite the tipi door."

She glanced at the structure that towered nearby, wondered what it was like inside, when she would be invited in, how long she would stay.

"Are you still married? Technically, or…"

"No. Not technically or any other way. You can't tie the knot from just one string."

"Well, you *can*, but…"

"All you'll have is a tangled string." He jacked one knee up for a forearm rest and eyed her frankly. "You be straight with me, I'll return the favor, and we'll get along fine."

"Look." She nodded toward the pen. No longer glued to the far side, the mustang peered at them. "He's listening to us."

"Sure feels like it." Logan wasn't looking at the horse directly. "He can't get away from us and he's too smart to beat himself up trying, so he's trying to put the pieces together. We don't eat grass, but we're not looking for horsemeat, either. We're not loud. We don't smell too dangerous. Maybe we got separated from our own herd and we're putting together a new band." He chuckled. "What should we call ourselves? Mary and the Contraries?"

"Clever. Just call me Mare."

"So that's what he smells." He glanced at her and smiled. "The Indian way, a contrary is like a clown. He does everything backward—the opposite of the way everyone else does. We traveled in bands, too, and there was always a *heyoka*."

"To entertain?"

"He makes people laugh, but it's really about balance. Everyone has a role to play." He nodded toward the pen. "Our boy understands this, probably better than we do."

"Are we assigning roles? Is that why he's listening?" She squared her shoulders, tucked her chin and lowered her voice. "Sound off when your role is called."

"He doesn't use words. Sometimes I think they hear thoughts."

"Oh, yes, dogs do, too. I know they do. They read people's minds."

"Deeper than that," he said. "They go deeper than the part of the mind that forms words. They don't read. They sense."

"Vibes?"

"Yeah, maybe. They're prey animals. They have to be sensitive to everything around them, be able to detect the slightest change in their surroundings. Sharp senses don't lie. We put it into words, we lose something. Or maybe we add something."

"You're using words right now. Are you losing or adding?"

"I don't know. I'm just sayin'." He chuckled. "I generally don't talk this much."

"Neither do I. I can control what I say, but those vibes…" He was moving closer. "Good thing most people have trouble sensing."

"Yeah. Good thing." He touched her chin, turned her face and kissed her softly. "Mary, Mary," he whispered.

"Never contrary." She closed her eyes and inhaled the spicy scent of sage and wood smoke. "I felt that coming."

"I felt wanted."

"I want—"

He hooked his arm behind her head and opened his mouth over hers and stole her next breath with the kiss she wanted, the kind that gave back and kept on giving. She welcomed him, her tongue touching his, her lips taking the measure of his. Full and moist, they took the lead in a sexy slow dance meant to bring more dancers to the floor, meant to get things going up and down their bodies, bundles of nerves dying to become entangled in utterly wild ways. In the end he touched his forehead to hers, and they mixed breath with breath and sigh with sigh.

"Good vibrations." He lifted his head. "Would you like to stay with me tonight?"

"It's not a good time."

He nodded and got to his feet. As soon as she started to follow suit, he offered her a hand. He didn't seem to mind the rejection, which was almost funny because she minded it very much. She touched his sleeve.

He slipped his arm around her shoulders and started walking her toward the round pen. Or her borrowed pickup—she wasn't sure which.

"It's complicated, Logan."

"No, it isn't." He gave her a little squeeze. "You gave me a straight answer. Don't tangle it up now." He gave a questioning glance. "Is there someone else?"

"No."

"Good." They reached the pen. He grabbed the top rail with his free hand and eyed the mustang. "We should come up with something to call him. We can change it later if we need to."

"Why would we need to?"

"It's a big commitment, accepting a name from someone. He might not be ready."

"How about Khaki?" She opted to take his point literally. "Isn't that a good name? You called him a claybank. It's a color we've all worn. You're wearing it now, and my khakis are never too far away."

"The color of dirt."

"Earth," she amended. "Good camouflage. We blend, like a proper band. It goes along with being quiet and unscented."

"You have a scent." He turned his nose to her hair. "It pleases me." He kissed her temple. "Even after you've gone."

"Yours is powerful. It attracts me." She closed her eyes and breathed deeply. "And stays with me."

"In a good way?"

"Oh, yes."

He nodded toward the mustang. "Earth on the outside, fire on the inside."

"And wind all around." She slipped her arm around his lean waist. "I used to think the prairie was monotonous. The same mile after mile. Sky, grass, rocks, dirt and wind all around. Until you run into the Black Hills, and then..." She flashed one thumb up.

"But now that I've been to places that seem to have even less variety, and I see all this through new eyes. Or older eyes and new perspective. There's more than meets the eye."

"I don't much like desert," he said.

"Grass is good. The deeper the roots, the better the sod."

"We'll take him out tomorrow," he decided. "Put him on grass."

"Let him go?"

"He's with us now." He lifted his voice and tried out the name. "Khaki." But he shook his head. "Uh-uh. That's not it."

"I know! Adobe!" The mustang's ears rotated forward. "He likes that better."

"I do, too." Logan squeezed Mary's shoulders. "Much better."

Chapter Five

Mary listened halfheartedly as she watched her mother stow the last of their grocery purchases in the refrigerator. Guilt dogged the better part of her heart, which was already halfway out the door and on its way back to its new desires. She'd had the good sense to decline Logan's invitation for a sleepover, but, *damn,* she was dying to get back out there. While Audrey chattered happily about the survival of her tomatoes thanks to Mary's timely weeding and watering, Mary counted the minutes. Now that her mother was in good spirits, had Mary done her duty for the day? *May I be excused now, Mother?* Mary was nothing if not dutiful, but suddenly duty couldn't hold a candle to desire, and her desire was to head for the hills.

Especially when her father invaded the kitchen, dragged a chair away from the table and made himself comfortable. "Is dinner ready?"

"It will be in just a few minutes." Audrey glanced at Mary and then at the clock as she hurriedly stowed staples—eggs, butter, juice—into the refrigerator. It was only eleven-thirty. Half an hour early. Father had always expected his main meal promptly at high noon. "We just got back from Hot Springs. I needed some things from the store, and Mary said—and she's right—might as well go the extra mile as long as she's driving and shop for what we'll need for—"

"It's dinner time. I came in to eat." He hauled himself out of the chair and shouldered his wife out of his way. "I don't have time for some big report."

"It'll only take me a minute to make you—"

"Get out of the way," he insisted. "I'll get it myself. You couldn't wait until Wednesday? I told you I wanted to go up to Rapid City on Wednesday." He looked like a turkey the way he craned his neck to get a bug-eyed peek at Mary over Audrey's head. "You've got your friend's pickup parked in the way out there."

"I was bringing in groceries."

"You've got Drexler property blocking access to *my* property."

"What in hell are you talking about?" Mary

shoved a handful of folded paper bags into a storage rack inside the broom closet. The days of her dancing to this man's tune were long over.

"Puts a bad taste in my mouth. Ruins my appetite." He ducked back down as Audrey backed away, cradling a carton of eggs. "Only taste I want in my mouth right now is..." He pushed a carton of cottage cheese to one side and swatted at a package of bagels. "You went to the store? What did you buy? I don't see any ring boloney. No summer sausage. What am I supposed to eat?"

"I got some smoked turkey, some ham, two kinds of bread. And I was going to make some—"

"Just stay out of the way." Brandishing a tube of liverwurst, he turned his scowl from his wife to his daughter. "You're supposed to be looking after her. She doesn't need to be running all over the country."

"I haven't been anywhere except the hospital in I don't know how long, Dan," Audrey said quietly.

"You don't need to go anywhere. You need to—"

"Don't yell at her." Mary returned her father's scowl. "I took my mother away from here for a few hours. If you have a problem with that, you can settle it with me."

"It's settled. I don't want her getting sick again." He dropped the liverwurst on a cutting board and pulled a slicer from the knife block. "I've got enough to worry about without her going down again." He took after the end of the tube of mashed meat with the point of the knife. "All she has to do is cook. That's all."

"And clean up your litter and take care of your laundry and your—"

"Not when she's sick. Are there any red onions around here?"

Mary imagined pulling her mother away from the pantry door, but she couldn't bring herself to add insult to injury. Her mother's very identity was at stake.

"That's why you're here, isn't it?" her father was saying. "Taking time off to look after your mother. That's what we thought, anyway." He held out his hand for the onion Audrey had fetched him. "I keep this place going, Daughter. I bought it, built it, kept it going with no end to the predators and little enough help. Regular meals is little enough to expect. That and loyalty." Poised to slice the onion, he pointed the knife tip at Mary. "You get yourself an Indian boyfriend, you'd better find out which side he's on."

"Dan," Audrey put in. "Please don't."

"Don't what? If I wanna yell in my own house, I'll yell." He threw a slice of onion on a piece of bread, added a thick slab of liverwurst, topped it with another piece of bread, smashed it down, snatched it up and slammed the back door on his way out.

Blessed silence.

"He's upset about that land," Audrey said quietly, as though he might be able to hear her from the yard. "The lawyer told him he can't sue." She gave a wan smile. "He's not himself."

"He's *exactly* himself," Mary insisted. No way would she keep her voice down. *Loud and proud.*

But her mother hadn't been to boot camp. "I want to be here with you, Mother," she said gently. "I meant to spend some time just hanging out, talking, getting you out of this house when *you* feel like going somewhere rather than…"

"It means the world to me, having you here. I know it isn't easy." Audrey glanced at the back door. "I know how you feel, Mary."

"Oh, Mother," Mary said, mimicking her adolescent not-so-loud, hardly-proud voice. She laughed. "You've always been able to read me like a book. I used to resent it, but now it's reassuring. Somebody gets me. I only wish I understood you better. I don't know why you stay."

"Where would I go?" Audrey ran her hand over the Formica countertop. She couldn't be in the kitchen five minutes without cleaning perfectly clean counters. "This is my house. Everything else is his, but not this house, no matter what he says."

Hey, Mary thought. That sounded almost loud and proud.

Her mother must have thought so, too, because her face brightened considerably. "You know, Crazy

Horse said, 'My lands are where my people lie buried.' Well, my house is where my children grew up."

"Crazy Horse, Mother?"

"I might not get out much, but I do read. And not just magazines." She was a magazine junkie. Subscriptions galore. Her eyes twinkled, as though she were holding a cookie behind her back. "I read actual books. I'll bet you didn't know that about me."

"Of course I did." Sort of. "I didn't know you were into history."

"Mr. Wolf Track is a kind man. I could tell, just by the way he—"

"Now, don't *you* start." Mary folded her arms and held off on a smile. For about five seconds. "Yes, he is. He is."

"And you really like him." Audrey waved off any thought of denial. "I'm still your mother, Mary."

"We've come a long way with the horse already. Did I tell you what we named him?"

"Adobe." Audrey sat down at the little kitchen table. "I do listen. You've taken the horse to heart. And maybe the man." She nodded as she gave Mary the take-a-seat signal. "He's different."

"I'm learning from them. I work with animals, too, but his way is about—" she smiled into her mother's loving eyes "—listening. Different how?"

"Different in your eyes. I don't know what you see, but I know you feel good about it and you want to see more." She leaned closer. "So *do it*. Give him a real chance."

"How do you know he wants a chance?"

Audrey smiled to herself. That enigmatic, *Mother knows* smile. Suddenly Mary wanted to jump across and get the truth out of the woman. *What do you know, and when did you know it, Mother? Are you that intuitive? Or are you just recycling used dreams?*

"Having you here has been good medicine for my heart," Audrey said. "I'm feeling stronger every day. You tell me about your dogs and now this wild horse, and you just light up. You talk about Mr. Wolf Track's way—"

"Logan."

"He's on the Tribal Council, Mary. He's an important man." Audrey reached for Mary's arm. "Don't hang around here too much. I want to see what you can do with that horse. Make a video."

"I'll take you to see him. And I'll take you anywhere else you feel like going." The cool feel of her mother's hand was a reminder of her reason for being there. "The army owes me some time off, and I'm spending it with my mother. I want to catch up. Talk the way we used to over chores. I'll be here for some canning. We should have cukes and beans before—"

"Mary." Her mother's hand lay dappled and slight on Mary's tanned forearm. "The best thing you can do for me is to follow your heart. When you left home years ago, you were running from heartache and it broke my heart. Not because you left—you did what was right for you—but because there was no way for me to ease the pain. That time was over for me. But you found your way, and I'm so proud of you."

"Nothing's over for you. I'm your daughter— always will be—and you're not expected to…" Help? She couldn't say that. Couldn't expect it, couldn't say she didn't expect it. "Give yourself credit. I'm here to tell you, Mother, you're stronger than you realize."

"I admire what you do." Again she leaned closer, as though she were confiding a secret pleasure. "I watch the animal shows on TV, and I see people training them for service, and I think, *that's what my daughter does*. We raise beef for—"

"For food, Mother. You produce food for people."

"Yes, I know." She squeezed Mary's arm. "I'm just so proud of you. I want to see what you do with your wild horse. I know it will be magical."

Mary smiled. "It'll be even more amazing than that. It'll be natural."

Mary didn't realize how fast her heart was set on the sight of Logan's pickup parked at the campsite until it fell into her gut midthump. There was a round pen, but no pickup. There was a tipi, but no Adobe.

There was a camp, but no fire. She was bearing down a dusty hillside under unrelenting blue sky and summer sun, and she was feeling chilled. She'd let the herd, *the family,* down and they'd gone off without her.

She called out for him anyway, ducked inside the tipi hoping to find him even though her keen senses told her the camp was empty. *Forgive us our trespasses.* Was it trespassing if you were family? How about if you'd been kissed? Not just kissed, but *really* kissed?

She felt strangely secure inside the canvas house, like a mouse taking shelter inside a brown paper bag. Logan's belongings surrounded her. His bedroll, several canvas bags and a folded tarp formed a neat row on one side of the tipi. On the other side a red Pendleton blanket with black and yellow geometric designs was draped over what appeared to be several boxes. A couple of towels were draped over a line strung between pine poles. At the back of the tent two traditional willow backrests looked as though they'd been set up for a tête-à-tête. The grass carpet had been tamped down, and the scent of sage filled the space.

She was tempted to try one of the backrests on for size or peek under the blanket and see if somebody'd left her some porridge, but a few minutes of static air and oppressive heat and she was watering the grass with the sweat rolling off her face. It was midsummer, and a tent in middle America felt no different from a tent in the Middle East in the middle of the day.

Tall grass swished against Mary's jeans as she made her way down to the creek. She knelt on the bank, splashed cool water on her face and let it sluice down her neck and into her bra. Then she braced her hands on her thighs and considered her next move. She wasn't going back to the house. *Mother's house.* Her mother had given her leave, and she was happy to take it. Relieved to leave the package she'd quietly purchased on their shopping trip, take another day. She didn't need the test. She knew what was going on inside her body. What she needed was to say it out loud. Make it real. *Say it loud and proud.* The din of unseen cicadas enveloped her. *Sound off with us, Tutan. Get real.*

She could stay and wait. She'd been invited the night before. *Would you like to stay with me tonight?* Which meant *sleep with me.* Which meant *have sex with me.* Which meant more than she would dare to show, more than he would ever know.

And she didn't know him. She didn't know his other life—his town, his job, his home, his family— and her curiosity had reached the tipping point. She wanted more of him. It was time to go looking for him. She'd start in Sinte.

The town of Sinte wasn't on the road to anywhere she'd generally needed to go. Growing up she'd lived next to Indian Country and rubbed elbows with its people, but she'd rarely ventured near its vital organs. The casino was a place where two worlds overlapped to form a kind of Disneyland for adults, but not for the Tutans, who had done family business in "white" towns. Mary wondered whether she would have felt less like a stranger if she had never been to Sinte at all. The old, unwelcome diffidence was creeping up on her as she parked the Drexler pickup and eyed the front doors of the tribal office building. *Get over it, Sergeant.* She imagined herself in uniform as she marched up to the reception desk wearing her game face.

Her request for Logan Wolf Track's office seemed to amuse the young woman sitting behind the desk. The glint in her dark eyes was a little intimidating.

"His office?"

"Is this the right building?"

"For the council, yeah. There's no meeting today."

"Do you know where I might find him?" The woman lowered her gaze and said nothing. "It's... he's training a horse with me. *For* me."

"She's come to see a man about a horse, Janine."

Mary turned to find a man wearing a badge standing behind her. He wasn't smiling, either. "Get back on the highway." He raised a hand to point the way. "Head west for a couple miles and look for a log house on the south side."

"Could be he has an office there," the woman said.
"Is there a sign?"

The woman almost smiled. "You mean, with his name on it?"

"It's the only log house out there," the man said. "You won't have no trouble finding it."

A tall, full cottonwood tree stood a few yards abreast of the small house in otherwise unbroken sod. The yard was immaculate—not a stray tool or toy or piece of trash in sight—and the only sign of human occupancy was the familiar pickup and horse trailer parked behind the house near a pine rail round pen twice the size of the portable one Logan had put up at camp. It was close to six feet high. There was a metal pole barn with an attached paddock and a small fenced pasture. Nothing fancy. Nothing proclaiming its owner to be "the best there is" among horse trainers.

He appeared at the top of a rise riding a flashy paint and ponying Adobe at the end of a long lead. Mary wasn't sure he saw her. She'd left the pickup in the sparsely graveled driveway and seated herself on the wheel housing on the shady side of the horse trailer. He varied the horses' gaits, taking an unhurried and indirect approach to the barn. The gate to the paddock stood open, and she made ready to close it behind rider and horses. On second thought, she stepped within the confines before securing the latch.

"I could've used your help loading him," he told her as he swung down from the saddle.

"You could've called me."

"Figured you were busy. How's your mom?"

"Doing well, thank you. I'm sorry you had to..." She noticed the halter Adobe wore for the first time. It appeared to be homemade. "It's like having a child, isn't it? Get a sitter or take him with you when you have to go somewhere."

"It was time to get him around another horse."

She stayed near the fence and watched Logan approach the mustang with a quiet word between them. One quick, deft pull on the end of some magical cowboy's knot and the halter fell away. Adobe jumped away, and Logan spoke to him again, his voice so low that Mary couldn't make sense of what he said. The two went separate ways as Logan led the saddle horse toward Mary. They exchanged the kind of smiles proud parents might share over baby steps.

"Next time he'll go easy," he said.

"And then we were four," she said, admiring the beautiful white paint with sorrel markings, including ears and a headband that looked like semaphores signaling from a snowbank.

"Not quite, but we're gettin' there. We had a good run." He handed Mary the reins, flipped the stirrup over the horn and loosened the cinch, talking all the while. "Hattie's instinct is to lead. Some might call her a Judas horse. I think of her as a bridge between two worlds."

"Different terms for different trainers?"

"Different way of thinking."

"I like yours." She rubbed her thumb over the supple rope rein. "What are these made of?"

"Horsehair. I make them myself."

"Is it part of the Indian way?"

He chuckled. "It's part of *my* way. That's called a *mecate*. An old *vaquero* put me onto this type of rein years back. Works great with the hackamore, which is the way I like to start horses."

"So your way isn't necessarily the traditional Indian way."

He gave her a growl and a scowl. "It is if I say it is." And then a smile and a wink. "I wrote the book."

"And you *stole* from the Spanish?"

"Hell, we stole the horses from the Spanish." He grinned. "And anybody else too slow to catch us. Sitting Bull said, take what's good from the immigrants and leave the rest." He lifted one shoulder. "I gave ol' Mario credit for being the one to teach me how to make them. Someday I'm gonna set up shop."

"Call it Mario's?"

"Callin' it Track Man's. Here's the logo." He made a hand creature, pinkie and forefinger raised as wolf ears, two middle fingers tapping the pad of his thumb as it wended its way in her direction in the style of the old video game.

She was mesmerized until the critter dove for her neck. She rewarded him with a girlish giggle. She had the presence of mind to keep it small for the sake of the horse.

"Do I have a winner?"

"With five-year-olds." She couldn't stop smiling like one. "You and my mother. She's quoting Crazy Horse to me today."

"I liked her right off." He pulled the saddle. "So you came looking for me."

"For my horse." She glanced at the pole barn. "This is a nice setup. Will we be moving our base camp?"

"We could." He glanced at her and nodded at the headstall. "Do we want to?"

She took the hint and removed the last of the paint's gear. "I like the back of beyond, but you're the one sleeping on the ground out there. What does Adobe say?"

"Ask him."

The mustang stood at the far end of the paddock, all ears. "He says you should try sleeping on your feet." Mary raised her eyebrows. "Oh, and if we promise to take him back to the sanctuary, he'll load right up."

"You hungry?" Logan followed her through the gate. "I've got a sister, wants to meet you."

"She knows about me? I mean..."

"I told her about you. Serving in the Middle East, among other things. Her son's over there."

"I'd love to meet her." She slid the lock. "What other things?"

"Nothing bad. Don't worry. She won't be gunning for you."

An X-ray technician, Logan's sister lived near the tribal office building in Indian Health Service housing. Logan waved at two children who were playing with a trio of roly-poly multicolored puppies in the fenced yard. The boy hollered "Hey, Lala Logan!" and hoisted a whimpering yellow pup overhead.

"Nice one," Logan called out as he opened the back door.

"He shouldn't do that," Mary said under her breath.

"They're my nephew's kids."

"What*ever*." She poked him in the side. "Didn't you hear the bitch growl?"

He turned and flashed a double take as he crossed the threshold. "I'm gonna go with *better her than me.* Hey, sis, I brought you a guest!"

Logan's sister, Margaret, was older, smaller and more gregarious than her brother. She offered hot coffee, cold tea and a sample of the fresh fry bread scenting her kitchen. She'd been expecting Logan, and it was clear that he never needed permission to bring a friend. She doted on him.

Her interest in Mary might have been merely an extension of her brother's—he introduced her as his *new partner*—but Mary had something else going for her. Like Margaret's son, she was a soldier. Mary traded service details with Margaret—outfits, posts, time served, universal complaints—without speaking of troublesome specifics.

"My son doesn't like that part of the world, but he doesn't mind the army," Margaret said as she refilled Logan's coffee cup. "He liked Germany. Says the people there really like Indians, especially the Sioux. So he was a big hero there. But now he's counting the days. I hope he doesn't get too lonesome, like my little brother did. He doesn't need to be hookin' up with—"

"What about those puppies you got outside?" Logan said. "Too old for soup, are they?"

Margaret patted her brother's shoulder. "Depends on who's cooking."

Mary rolled a small bite of chewy bread from one cheek to the other, her gaze from one face to the other. "You're kidding, right?"

"Mary's a dog trainer," Logan said.

"You train them to find bombs?"

"I train for lots of jobs, but sniffing for explosives is maybe the most important one right now."

"Maybe you trained the one that saved my son's

unit." Margaret glanced at Logan. "Did he tell you about that? One of those dogs found a bomb in a kid's toy. Can you believe that?" She gave Mary a knowing smile. "We don't eat dogs."

"Not anymore," Logan said, and Margaret punched his shoulder. "Okay, sis, jeez. Probably not since—" he caught her warning glance "—the turn of the century. I know I've never tasted it." He smiled at Mary. "Have you ever tasted horsemeat?"

She shook her head. "Not that I know of. Which century?"

"Which*ev*er," he said, imitating her. "Somewhere in the world somebody's eating horsemeat as we speak. And that somebody is not Lakota."

"You make a good pair," Margaret said. She grinned as her gaze ping-ponged between them. "A good pair."

The back door burst open, and the two children scurried inside. The boy carried the pup he'd shown off in the yard, and the girl followed with an eye patch pup under one arm and a squirmy black one under the other.

"Keep those dogs outside," Margaret ordered.

"But Lala Logan…"

"I'll be out in a minute, Teddy." The kids did an about-face and zipped out the door singing an *okay* duet. "Teddy and Selina," Logan told Mary. "They live next door, more or less."

"It's nice that you can help out while their dad's overseas."

"Third tour," Margaret said. "Selina just turned five, and she hardly knows him."

"A military career can be hard on families these days," Mary said.

"My son's in the Guard." Margaret lifted one shoulder. "He's grown up a lot. I'll say that." She craned her neck for a peek out the window. "They're standing there waiting for you, little brother."

Logan liked to give Teddy and Selina special attention. Their dad had been gone too long, but he was serving honorably. The kids wondered whether Randy was ever coming back to stay, and Logan wondered sometimes, too. The boy had seemed distant the last time he'd been home.

Logan knew that faraway look, the one that settled in a person's eyes when she felt like she was missing some excitement somewhere. Some people cut the ties gradually and started drifting. Others hacked into them all at once and bolted. Logan rarely thought about his wife anymore except in connection with the boys. Randy's wife and his mother were making up for his absence, and the kids were thriving. Logan had stayed angry too long. If he had it to do over again, he'd start by separating Tonya's eyes from the boys'. They were not the sum total of two people who'd skipped out on them. They were his sons.

And the woman who knelt in the grass between

them was his new partner. She laughed when Salina called her "Lala's girlfriend." She'd really laugh when she found out what *lala* meant. Leave it to kids to cut to the chase, he thought as he watched Mary show the children how to hold the puppies. She pointed out that they all had different personalities.

"I'll bet this one will be a good fetcher," she said of the black. "The quiet one might be a sniffer. What do you have in your pocket, Teddy?" The yellow pup was determined to find out.

"I don't know." He plunged his hand inside. "Oh, yeah, beef jerky. We get to keep one, and one of our cousins wants one, so there's one more left. If you want one, you can take the boy."

"One bitch is enough," little girl echoing what she'd clearly been told. "Or else we have to get rid of Peaches."

"Sounds like your mom laid the law down. You should be able to have Peaches spayed just as soon as everyone's weaned." And it was about time. Peaches needed an ally in that regard.

"I'll take care of it," Logan said. "If you keep one of the pups, I'll take them both in. Which cousin are you talking about?"

"Maxine. So we get to keep one?"

"That's up to Grandma, and Maxine's dad has to take care of Maxine's puppy. I'm just helping you guys out."

"Like you always do, Lala Logan." Teddy nodded

at the black puppy. "So you can have the boy if you want. Boys are easier to train."

"Where'd you get that idea?" Mary took the yellow dog from Selina. "Let me show you how smart this girl is." Within a few minutes—and with the help of Teddy's beef jerky—Mary taught the puppy to sit by applying pressure to the scruff of her neck, reminding the kids that this was where Peaches picked them up.

"She likes you," Salina said. The puppy nuzzled Mary's hand.

"She knows she can trust me. That's the first thing an animal wants to know about you. Are you going to hurt it? Are you going to feed it?" She laughed as she cuddled the dog to her breast. "Oh, yes, I'd gladly take you with me, but I can only have one dog where I live, and that has to be my partner." She glanced up at Logan. "My *canine* partner."

"You've got all kinds of partners," Logan observed quietly.

"Peaches is part police dog. You could make her puppy an army dog."

"We don't take puppies. In six months, eight months, if I'm still…" She ruffled the fur on top of the puppy's head and made its ears flop like two babies waving bye-bye. "Yeah, you'd make some MP a fine partner, wouldn't you?"

"That would be so cool," Teddy said. "You could

keep him for her until he's old enough to go in the army, Lala."

"One deal at a time."

She waited until they were back at his place loading the horse before she asked the burning question. "Is Lala a nickname?"

"Sort of. It's short for *tunkasila*."

"Which means?"

"Grandfather." The look on her face made him smile. "My sister's their grandmother."

"But your sister's a lot older than you."

"So? What does age matter?" He looked her in the eye. "Do *you* mind them calling me Lala?"

"Well, no. I mean…"

"Or calling you Lala's girlfriend?"

She glanced away. "They're kids. Kids use all kinds of names for their relatives. But, really, you're their uncle. *Great* uncle."

As if that meant something. Kids, grandpas, girlfriends, older, younger…what the hell did any of it mean? How different were they, anyway?

"What's a great uncle? Better than a good one?" He gave a perfunctory smile. "I don't claim we're doing it exactly as we always have, but traditionally there were no cracks for our kids to fall through. Anthropologists call it extended family. They draw charts with circles and arrows to explain what they call a complex system."

"It does sound a little complicated."

"It's life. It's the way we live. It became complicated when they tried to make us live differently. Not just with the reservation system, but when they took our kids so they could get religion or training or new parents, whatever they thought we should be trading our way of life for—well, they pulled the rug out from under us, our whole foundation. Nearly destroyed us." He gestured impatiently. "Hell, you grew up just down the road from us. You must know."

"I should know more," she said quietly. "I should know a whole lot more."

"You had your own life. It's understandable." He closed the trailer door and slid the bolt. "For a kid."

"Funny how you have to go away for a while, see a little bit of the world, and when you come back you realize nothing's really changed but it all looks different."

"Because you've changed?" He searched her eyes. "I didn't know you before, so I'm just asking."

"I feel different."

"How's that?"

He needed to know. He liked her. He liked her so much it was beginning to bother him. Bother his mind at odd times. And even times. Bother his deep down inner core almost all the time.

"I'm not scared." She said it as though it should come as a surprise, as though it was even news to her. "I know I can handle myself, do what needs to be done, what's right. What's right for me."

"Hard to imagine you any other way."

"Because you didn't know me before. And I lived right down the road and didn't know you."

"Twenty miles and ten years difference." He put his hand up to his ear. "Can you hear me now?"

She laughed. "Loud and clear."

He looked at her for a moment, smiling up at him, making him feel different. Not different in years or experience or even lifestyle, whatever that meant. Just different from the way he'd felt a week ago.

He put his arm around her shoulders. "Then let's lock and load."

Chapter Six

"Hey, Sal!" Mary crossed paths with a calico cat as she let herself into the Drexler house through the mudroom. "Do we want the cat out?"

"Only if we have something against birds," Sally called out from the kitchen.

"Come back here, kitty." Too late. Taking to the grass, the calico was on the prowl. "No meadow-larks!" Mary called after her as she closed the screen door.

She greeted Sally in the kitchen with a wave of her digital camera. "I took some pictures of the camp. Can we download them on to your computer? Maybe there's something in here you can use." She winced. "Does she really hunt birds?"

"Every time somebody lets her out. She's supposed to be a house cat. I'm trying to get her to acquire a taste for mouse. Coffee?"

"Love some. I'll take one of those muffins, unless they're already spoken for." She grabbed a cup from the cabinet and a napkin from the wooden holder Sally had made in eighth grade shop class. Mary had made one just like it. She'd given it to her mother and hadn't seen it in years. Hidden away, probably. Mother never threw anything out, but if it prompted her husband's disapproval, it disappeared.

"Take two. They're small." Sally led the way through the living room, walking with a noticeable hitch in her step. "Come on. I want you to tell me everything while we download." She turned, grinning as she backpedaled. "You named the mustang Adobe. Love that. You've been hanging out. You've already started training him. The horse, not the man. This isn't boot camp. You have to be subtle."

"When is it going to be my turn?"

"Jump in anytime." She started plugging the camera into her system and went on talking. "I knew you two would hit it off. Not that I know Logan all that well, but I couldn't just… Oh, these are good." Sally pointed to a small chair on wheels as she rolled her armed and adjustable office chair closer to the computer display. "This is great. Can I use these?"

"I was hoping you'd be able to use them. I got the camera at the PX two months ago, and I'm still learning how to use it. Are they any good?" Mary scooted in close to watch the slide show of the tipi from all angles standing tall and timeless against the horizon, the sky spreading its morning and evening mantles over the camp, sunlight flashing in the creek and the claybank mustang—the star attraction. Yes, they were good.

"It's beautiful out there. It's like stepping back in time. Very peaceful. I really just want to stay out there and be peaceful, you know? Real R and R. Leave time. Take leave of everything *but* my senses." She laid her hand on Sally's slight shoulder. "Sounds a little too Zen for South Dakota, doesn't it?"

"I don't know Zen from Obi-Wan Kenobi, but it sounds Lakota." Sally turned, suddenly aglow. "I think I might be getting married."

"When?"

"We've been talking about it a lot." Sally rolled her eyes and sighed. The glow dimmed. "But I don't know if it's fair to Hank. I've had a really good run these last few months, but the monster is sucking on my nerves again. I went down on one knee the other night, and Hank said it was about time I proposed."

"Nice guy."

"I know. Stupid to let one like that get away." She tipped her head back against the headrest. "But I think we should wait. I want him to know what he'd be getting into."

"It doesn't matter, Sally. He's a good man, and he loves you."

"Oh, come on, that's so 'Hollywood.'" Sally smiled again. "But I do enjoy a feel-good movie once in a while and Hank makes me feel wonderful and I haven't scared him off yet but if I wait around long enough…" She took a breath. "I don't want to wait."

"Sounds like he doesn't either."

"He says he's ready any time." Sally glanced at the computer screen. "He's gone a lot with his job as a rodeo medic. A show here, three shows over there." Three tipi shots rolled past. "But I think it could work. He wouldn't have to be around me all the time, you know? I can be pretty hard to live with." She laughed. "Just ask my sister."

"Where is Cheekers, anyway?" Mary grimaced. She'd uttered the *C* word. Poor Ann.

Poor Ann? She'd shaped up, studied up, kept up with a teaching job and a ranching operation and met up with a wonderful man. Of course, the man was icing on the cake. Cake was fine without icing. Marry him, don't marry him, life could be good either way. It was all in the attitude.

"She's supervising volunteers down at the barn. Zach's hauling in hay."

"You have a lot going on here, Sally. Maybe Hank wants to be part of it."

"Oh, he absolutely is. He's a terrific ferrier. He's

great with the horses. He's, you know...he's used to traveling all over the place, which is great. It's exciting. I used to be a rodeo stock contractor before the MS, and then..." Sally gestured expansively. "Well, *you* know. How much down time does it take before you start feeling antsy?"

"Does Hank seem antsy?"

"Not so far. He goes on the road when it's time, does his job." She tucked her hand under her chin and smiled dreamily. "And then he comes back to me. But we've only been together—"

"He strikes me as a man who knows his own mind." Mary drew a deep breath. "Which is enviable."

"Can you come? It won't be a big fuss, but we always said we'd stand up for each other. I'll toss you the bouquet." Sally's brow suddenly furrowed. "You're not doing another Middle East tour anytime soon, are you?"

"Who knows these days?" A month ago she would have said she was ready, willing and able to go where the army needed her. It should've been rolling off her tongue now.

"Are you tired of it?"

"*Tired* wouldn't be quite the word, Sally. I like the work. I'm good at it. It's not like I have any trouble going where they send me." Mary laid her hand on Sally's jeans-clad thigh. "When you get married, I want to be there. So stop fooling around. You've got three weeks."

"That's what Hank told me when he signed on to help out here. *You've got three weeks.*" Sally waggled her eyebrows. "And then we started fooling around."

"That's a nice one, isn't it?" Mary smiled as she watched the screen. "Look at those colors."

"Mmm-hmm. Lovely place to take leave of everything but your senses."

"*I'm* not fooling around." *Not me.* Not straight-laced Mary. Not buttoned-down Sergeant Tutan.

"Of course not. You're R-and-R-ing. All I have to say is, rock on, girlfriend." Sally rocked back in her fancy computer chair. "I still need more qualified applicants for the challenge. We want twenty-five top-notch competitors. I'm not getting the word out enough, I guess. Either that or horse people aren't mostly flat broke these days. But unless all them high-pollutin' horseless carriages get recalled, I see horse prices going up," Sally drawled. "Still, I'm pretty sure it's the promo thing. I want good people. Not just horse lovers, but people who really understand horses and can see all kinds of potential for *these* horses."

"I can think of one guy who might be interested. Indian guy from Wyoming. He said he was going home to his horses after he got his discharge. I have his address."

"Call him," Sally ordered.

"I said *address*. It's a P.O. box."

"Not that many addresses in Wyoming. Indian Country narrows it down. Plus, he's horse people." She sang a chorus of *"It's a Small World After All."*

Mary laughed. "Okay, I'll see what I can do."

"Ask Hoolie to help. It amazes me what he can find on the Internet." Shifting in her chair, Sally turned serious. "How would Logan feel about competing against his son?"

"His son applied?"

She leaned back and grabbed a paper from her gray "In" box. "Ethan Wolf Track," she read dramatically. "Very interesting résumé." Sally paused, ostensibly for effect, but she was on her way to another part of her mental map. "You realize how little contact we had with the people on the reservation when we were kids? Except when we played them in sports. And we're—"

"Right down the road, I know. My father had Indians working for him."

"Your father has a big operation."

"*Had*. It's shrinking."

Sally glanced away. "I'm…"

"Don't say you're sorry, Sally. Not to me. You know how I feel. I love what you're doing."

"Not because it hurts your father."

"Nothing hurts him. He's untouchable. No, he doesn't need all that land." Mary stared at the paper in Sally's hand. "Logan hasn't said much about his sons. If he's qualified, what does it matter how Logan feels about it? You need contestants."

"The statement of purpose—you know, that little essay you had to write?" Sally turned the page over. "Ethan's is pretty interesting. Sounds like he's a real bad boy. Or *was*." Sally glanced at the computer screen. The tipi faded into a picture of Logan and Adobe facing each other off. "I don't know. I owe Logan, for sure."

"Why don't you ask him?" Mary had taken the picture from Logan's viewpoint, the side of his chiseled face, his straw cowboy hat, his strong shoulders in the foreground framing the majestic black and khaki mustang. His viewpoint was clear where the horse was concerned. But people? He spoke little of his adopted sons.

"Ask which?" Sally said.

"Logan. He came to see Hank."

"Logan's outside?" Sally clasped her hands behind her head and smiled. "Well, that should be interesting. So is his son."

Logan found Hank loading his pickup topper with the tools of the horseshoeing trade, which he pursued in his spare time. Just the hat Logan wanted to find his friend wearing. But the hat on the man he was acquainting with his blacksmith shop in a pickup was even more familiar. Logan had given the hat to his younger son years ago. The brim was crinkled and the crown had been crushed, but it had held up pretty good. *Man, if that hat could talk.*

Rangy, rugged and built more like a running back than a cowboy, Logan's son looked nothing like the man purported to be his father. He didn't look much like his mother, either. He was his own man, come hell or high water. Ethan had explored both.

Hank saw Logan coming and quietly stepped aside.

"Hello, Ethan."

Ethan nodded. "Logan."

"You don't look surprised."

"Neither do you." Ethan gave a slow smile and an even slower-in-the-making handshake. "Twenty thousand dollars is a lot of money."

"Damn right it is. And two years is a long time." *Let it go. Take his hand, and let the rest go.*

"I've been busy since I got out. Working in a rehab program."

"How long do you have to rehab?"

"I said I was *working*. I get paid to work with horses, just like you do."

"You rehabbing horses, or people?"

"Somebody once told me horses don't need rehabbing if you start 'em right."

"I'm just askin'. It's two different things, but either way..." Studying the scuffed toes of his son's boots, Logan nodded. "Good for you, either way, Ethan. You're gonna get into this, then?"

"Thinkin' about it. I filled out the papers."

"Have you talked to Trace lately?"

"About a week ago. He's the one who told me about the mustang challenge." Ethan's boot heels scraped the gravel as he shifted his center of gravity from one to the other. "Sounds like he's doin' good."

Eyes focused on distant hills, Logan nodded again. Trace was a good boy. He didn't come home much, but he always let Logan know where he was. Made a pretty good living as a rodeo cowboy. Took Logan's expired dream and gave it new life. But this was Ethan. Enough said about Trace.

"Who's this?" Ethan nodded past Logan's shoulder and smiled. "She's looking for somebody. I'm guessin' it's you."

Logan drew a deep breath. He could've used a little more icebreaking time with his prodigal son.

"Mary, this is my son, Ethan." The two greeted each other with a handshake. "Mary and I are in this together. She's got the horse, and I've got all the rest."

"He's not always this modest." Ethan turned on the charm. He'd always had it, and Logan was glad to see that hadn't changed. "You hooked up with the right man, Mary."

Mary tugged on the brim of her baseball cap, adjusting it against the sun. "I'm sure he taught you everything he knows."

"Not quite." Logan fought the urge to lay his hand

on his son's shoulder. He could just see Ethan shrugging away the way he'd started to when he was about ten. "I've learned a lot since he was last home, so he's got a few years' catching up to do."

"I've learned a few things myself." Ethan folded his arms. "So you've already got a horse. Guess I'm already behind schedule, huh?"

"I think everyone gets the same amount of time. We wanted to get started right away. I'm on leave from the army."

"Hooah," Ethan barked. "I did my time with them, too. What outfit?"

"I'm a dog handler."

"MP?" He laughed. "Man, I can't get away from you guys."

"Mary actually trains dogs. Handlers, too, right?" Mary nodded, and Logan went on. "She's been in Iraq. Afganistan. Where else?"

"I grew up here. Mary *Tutan*." She gestured northward. "My parents live—"

"Tutan, yeah. I know that name." Ethan nodded, considering each face in turn. "And you're working with Logan Wolf Track. Now that's some strange bedfellowship."

"Ethan…"

"What? I said *ship*." He switched the kid away from Logan and turned the man to Mary. "No offense intended. I haven't been around too many women in the last, uh, half my life."

"Don't worry, Ethan. I've forgotten how to take offense. You did hear him say I've spent half my life in the army." She flashed a pretty smile. "And I've been a woman the whole time."

"Bet that's not easy."

"It's not easy no matter who you are," Mary said. "Hardest job you'll ever love, right?"

Ethan chuckled. "And you get no love back."

"Oh, I solved that problem. I got a dog."

"I like her. She's quick on the draw. A real Jane Wayne." Ethan tapped Logan's chest with the back of his hand. It felt almost like a hug. "You sure this old man can keep up with you? He's probably old enough to be your father."

And *that* felt like a slap in the face. "We're training a horse, Ethan."

"Oh, I don't know." Grinning, Ethan scanned the treetops behind the barn. "I feel some electricity in the air, and there's not a cloud in the sky."

"Damn," Logan muttered under his breath.

"See, this is why I don't call. My dad's a big Indian, and I'm a little Indian."

"Meaning he talks a good game," Logan said.

"Meaning you're the chief, and I'm not much Indian." He raised his hand, palm up. "If they approve me for the competition, I might…" He saw Hank heading for the barn, and he leaned in that direction. "I'll catch up with you," he promised Logan. Or Mary.

Logan took the promise for himself. "If you need anything, you know where to find me."

"He always says that." Ethan flashed Logan a million dollar smile. "And I never need anything."

Mary stood by Logan's side and put her hand on the small of his back. Absorbing his tension, she slowly pressed the heel of her hand into the muscle. He didn't seem to notice.

"It's been two years since you've seen him?" she asked as they watched Ethan approach Hank with an exchange of words that did not carry beyond the two men.

"About that."

"He wants to please you."

He looked at her as though she had her head on backward.

"Trust me. He doesn't think he can, so he doesn't try. That song and dance wasn't for me. It was for you."

He glanced away shaking his head. He was hurting, and she couldn't think of any way to help. She kneaded his back gently, the way she'd learned to calm a dog after an explosion. It was more than an affront. It was a feeling of failure. *I did something wrong. That shouldn't have happened.*

"I got what I needed here," he said finally. "Did you?"

"Sally talked a mile a minute while she took the pictures off my camera. She needs more participants for Mustang Sally's Makeover Challenge. So, if you know anybody who might be interested..."

"I'm not a recruiter." He jerked his head, indicating his pickup. "You coming?"

His first glimpse of the lodge poles reaching for the sky dissolved the knot in Logan's gut. The mustang was glad to see him. He hadn't wanted to leave the horse alone, but Mary had jumped in the pickup with him, her eyes looking all needy like she had something on her mind, so he hadn't said anything. Turned out she hadn't said anything either. He figured she wanted to use the phone or the bathroom or talk something over with Sally. She hadn't said anything on the way back, and that was fine, too.

And so was Ethan. Healthy, looked like he'd packed on some muscle, hadn't done anything crazy to himself like tattoo himself up like some kind of billboard or shave his head. Didn't look like he was doing anything to jack himself up. Good to know.

"He's looking good," Logan said, adding quickly, "Adobe. He knows the pickup, knows it's us."

"He's not afraid of us anymore."

"No, but he still doesn't understand what we're about. We're getting there, though."

"It feels good when you make that connection."

"Yeah."

They left the pickup, and she surprised him by slipping her hand into his as they walked toward the round pen. He wasn't used to holding hands. He wouldn't have taken her for a handholder, either, but it felt good. Like *that connection.* He gave her hand a little squeeze—where had *that* come from—and she returned the pressure with interest. And they both laughed.

Adobe looked at them as though they were a pair of prairie dogs. You could break your neck if you stepped into one of their holes, but in the flesh they were turning out to be pretty harmless.

"Ethan's the kind of guy who'll play tag with thunderbolts," Logan told her. "Acts like he's not afraid of anything. We've butted heads a few times, as you could probably tell."

"He's been in trouble?"

"Big time." He folded his arms over the top rail of the pen. "He wasn't cut out for the military. Uniform fit too tight. Came home lookin' for a fight and found it with the law." He glanced at her, gave a deferential nod. "And the law won."

"Did anyone get hurt?"

"He did. Did two years for messin' with the wrong woman. 'Course, stealing her daddy's car was the formal charge." He nodded. "He's like that horse. Strong and beautiful on the outside, sensitive as hell on the inside."

"I wouldn't say Ethan looks like a prey animal."

"Does this boy look like prey?" He was taking the horse's measure. "Look at the muscle on this guy. He could run you down and smash your head in like a melon. But that's not who he is."

"You're talking to a soldier, Logan. A lifer, in fact. I know the difference between predator and prey. Adobe's cautious, as well he should be."

He turned to her. "Are *we* afraid of us?"

"There's nothing to be afraid of, is there? We're not operating strictly on instinct. We've got our…" She made a rolling what's-the-word gesture.

"Yeah, that's workin' for us." He looked at her speculatively. "Are you a lifer?"

"I like what I'm doing." She nodded convincingly. "I really do, and I'm *good* at it, which surprised me at first. I never thought I'd earn a living working with animals."

"You like knockin' around from post to post?"

"I did at first." End of discussion. Suddenly she had her foot on the rail, and she was set to scale. "It's my turn to go in there alone. You coach me." He reached for her arm, but she was already swinging her leg over the top of the fence. "No, I'm good. Seriously. Nothing to fear."

"If you're afraid, back off."

"I'm not." She rubbed her hands over the back pockets of her jeans. Adobe stood quietly. "Neither is he. Tell me what to do."

"Stay where you are." Logan went to the pickup and came back with a duffel bag. He reached through the fence and handed her a coiled rope. "Get him moving. Be the center of his circle."

Mary used the tasseled end of a cotton rope to cause a stir in Adobe's limited world. She kept him moving, made him keep his distance from her, calmly convinced him of her authority. She could feel the difference between the mustang's nature and that of a dog. As she adjusted she could feel herself opening up in new ways.

"He's ready to trust you," Logan said quietly from behind the fence. She let the rope slide from her fingers and tuned her ears into the man's voice even as she directed the sum of her awareness toward the horse. "Let him come to you now. Turn away a little. Don't turn your back. A quarter turn, like you want your kid to follow you. 'Come with me. Let's go this way.'" She drew a long, slow breath as the animal approached. "Sweet," Logan said, and she smiled and took a step to see whether he'd follow. "Steady. You're the lead mare now. Slow, sure, steady."

Adobe worked his tongue and his jaw as though he had a mouthful of hot-off-the-griddle feed. He followed closely until, of her own accord, Mary slowed to a standstill. The horse took one more step and snuffled at her shoulder. Then he took another step and lowered his head in front of her. There he stood, his cheek a hair's breadth from touching her belly, his ear becoming a funnel for her breath.

He knew her secret. She'd been keeping it locked

up so tight inside, she hardly knew it was there. Adobe wanted to put her at ease with it. She didn't have to tell anyone or justify anything or make any decisions. But she had to recognize the fact that her womb was not empty. The connection between them felt like a transfusion of pure energy. Somehow she was drawing courage from the horse's conviction. It was neither a good time nor a bad time. It simply *was*. She could stop looking for a flow of blood that wasn't coming, stop dissing and dismissing the changes in her body and start believing any time now. She was all female, and there was no better source of strength than the organic stuff that made her so.

Adobe—salt of the earth—knew her secret. Amazing. He had her number, and it was no longer one.

Logan was transfixed. He was a big believer in the *wakan* aspect of *sunka wakan*. Literally translated, the horse was "sacred dog," an irony that was not lost on him as he watched Mary and Adobe come to terms. He had experienced what he was witnessing— a true empathetic osmosis with a horse—only once, and it had changed his outlook on just about everything. An old saddle horse had taken him from a dark place in his life into the light. He'd known that horse since he was a kid, but what he hadn't understood was how well the horse knew him, knew he still had something in reserve. Tonya had taken the pickup and left him with two kids and a horse. He'd left the kids alone in the house and tried to go after her on the horse. Crazy.

Thank God for horse sense.

But this was different. This horse was wild. What was happening between Mary and Adobe was as purely empathetic as anything he'd ever seen. Whatever it was about, it was solely theirs. He couldn't say how long they stood together. There was no fear. They were both relaxed, easy, free to stay or go. When she spoke, it was for the pair of them.

"He'll take the halter now."

"Too soon," Logan said. He was the coach, after all.

"Let me try. I can't explain it. It's a feeling. I have a good feeling about it."

Unable to feel whatever it was, he wanted to pull her away. But this was her call. He had a gut full of butterflies, but there was no doubt in his mind. He approached with great care, handed her the halter and watched her slide the nylon strap over the horse's nose and lift it over his ears. He had not raised his head far from her middle. She moved with amazing confidence.

"He'll take me on his back now." She glanced at her partner and smiled. "How about a leg up?"

There was no tension in the look she gave Logan. No challenge, no mind over matter. She had nothing to prove.

"I want you to drape yourself over his back for a moment first. Let him feel your weight. If he's going to jump away, your feet will be near the ground."

"He won't jump away," she said. "He gets me completely."

Initially she complied. Adobe stood calm, adjusting to the sack of warm flesh and fine bone draped over his back.

And then Mary took it upon herself and her strong arms and legs to lift, shift and straddle him. It was a beautiful thing to watch. Logan drew a deep, soundless breath. Whatever the animal got about the woman, mutual trust came with it. No questions asked.

She inched forward, settled behind the horse's withers and formed a cinch with her legs. With a roll of her hips she impelled him to walk. When she slipped slightly, Adobe stopped smoothly. She helped herself to a handful of black mane, centered herself, and gave another subtle hip roll, affecting a sensuous tightening in Logan's groin. He swallowed hard, leaving him feeling dry and needy. His whole being wanted quenching.

Adobe arched his neck and started forward again, easing unfettered from a walk to a gentle canter, and Mary's eyes shone with wonder. Logan was mesmerized. She had made the horse hers, and now she would have the man. Adobe brought her to him, and she slid into his arms. He kissed her, fiercely claiming her, and she claimed him right back.

And now it was his call.

Chapter Seven

The agreement was wordless. It was made eye to eye and hand to hand with the taste of want and willingness on their lips. They walked side by side—his arm around her shoulders, hers around his waist—no question in her mind, no hesitation in his step. He lifted the flap over the tipi door, and she ducked inside and found his bed spread before her. She sat down to take off her boots, and he did the same, casting off two in the time it took her to pull off one. He cocked her half a smile, took her heel in hand, gave a quick jerk and tossed her boot over his shoulder. Then he backed her down to the mat with a kiss.

She gave herself over to wanting him. Her mouth received his eagerly, gave back fervently, and she found it almost as good to give as it was to receive. Her fingers went for his shirt buttons and discovered snaps. He smiled against her mouth when she popped the first one open. The rest came apart like zipper teeth. She laid hands on his smooth bronze chest, touched his flat nipples with her thumbs until they were flat no more. She kept it up until he groaned. She moved her legs apart, just enough to give him perch, a ready foxhole for his pleasure and protection. He widened the berth with his thighs and began nudging at the narrows. Ah, the fox was growing, coming into its own. Hard and heavy and insistent, it nudged and prodded and promised to please, if only someone would let it out and take it in.

Mary slid her hand between them, tucked it into the waistband of his jeans and found a brass button and a tight buttonhole rather than the quick snap she'd imagined. His knowing chuckle rumbled in his throat as he nibbled his way down the side of her neck.

"What's your hurry?"

"No talk," she ordered. Words formed thoughts, and thoughts were dead weight. "All action," she insisted.

He rucked up her T-shirt and ran into her bra, which he dispatched single-handedly. He braced himself on one hand and used the other to touch, tracing the outer curve of one breast, the inner flat of the other. His thumb circled a nipple, closing in slowly. He watched it do what she felt it doing, but she felt more than he could possibly see, especially when his thumb reached its goal and touched barely, rubbed softly, took on the help of his forefinger and made a molehill on top of a mountain. She was tender there. She was burning there. A tiny bit of tender tinder, a match head bursting into flame. His mouth should have smothered it. His tongue should have drenched it, but he only added fuel. She drew a sharp, shaky breath when he moved his mouth to her dry nipple and applied his sandpaper thumb pad to the wet one.

He kissed his way down to her belly button, unbuttoned, unzipped and undid, nibbling her inner thighs, nuzzling between her legs in a way that gave unthinkable pleasure. No dead weight. Nothing to hold her down when he bid her come without speaking the earthbound word. She felt giddy and weak when he led the way in the peeling off, the sliding together, the firm fox darting fearlessly into a new place, a white-hot dark place that had a life of its own.

She tasted her secret self on his tongue, her inner life, her brackish core. She tasted him, too. His shoulder smacked of power. His neck tasted like tenderness. His face was warm and tangy, like sunshine. She was one with him, one surge, one rush, one river flowing, even as he held his own, pushed her past him and kept her going and going, toying with her like a balloon—bump and drift, bump and drop, bump bump bump and *whoosh*. They held together, careening around a fantastic hairpin curve, shuddering with the speed and the force and the impact, and finally floating woozy and feather light back to the ground.

Mary coasted on the easy in and out of her lover's breathing, the steady lub-dub in his chest, the slick feel of his skin, and the essential scents of earth and sage and musk and sex. It was all in her head. No room for anything else. She wasn't tired. She was simply sated, and so she slept.

She rolled over and found him sitting back on his heels and snapping his jeans. He smiled at her as he tucked one hand deep into his waistband and zipped up with the other.

"Leaving already?" She smiled lazily. "Oh, right. This is your place."

"I'll be right back. I'm just gonna turn some air on us for the next round."

"What are you going to plug into?"

"A sweet little generator that I can crank up by hand." He tucked back a bit of hair that had slid over her eye. "But that's just me. The air moves on its own."

"You're funny." She shifted to her back. "Did we sleep together?"

"You're a sound sleeper."

"Not unless I've had a good workout first. You're very good for an older man."

"With age comes staying power."

She frowned. "Did I make any noise?"

"You were so still and quiet, I had to check to make sure you were breathing." He brushed the backs of his fingers over the side of her face. "Slept so hard, you've got some rack burn."

She rubbed her cheek, but there was no erasing bed face. She probably looked as though she'd walked into a screen door. "How long...what time is it?" She rotated her bare wrist. Nothing but a couple of freckles. "Where's my watch?"

"Somebody must've stolen it while you were sleeping."

"Well, now I feel naked." She smiled as she swept her fingers across her chest. "Better keep your pistol primed, partner."

"That'll be your job." He cocked a finger and thumb gun at her and winked. "Partner."

Oh, he was cool.

Lord, he looked good walking away.

Mary lay on his bed watching a white cloud pass among the poles that thrust through the smoke hole and reached for the sky. All around her bit by bit the canvas wall climbed the poles from the ground up. She turned her head to the side and watched the long, lean pair of blue jeans move through the crisp grass and thought about the strong legs they clothed, the way she had wrapped hers around his and then around his slim waist and over his sturdy shoulders as though he were a piece of gymnastics equipment. She had lost her ever-lovin' mind, and it had felt right. As long as no complications were voiced, none existed.

He'd used a condom. She liked the way he'd handled that particular move. No discussion, no fumbling around, no excuses. No filling her with anything but wonder.

No making her feel like a dumb ass because she assumed that once the thing was on it was going to stay on the whole time. The last time she was with a man, it hadn't. And no, she hadn't been on the pill. Not that the soldier had asked, not even in passing. Why would she be? She wasn't in a relationship. If she needed a little recreation, she went to the gym. The only pick-up game she ever got into involved a basketball. One time. One miserable, lonely night with a soldier passing through her life on a three-day pass.

Stop it, Mary. Turn off the tape. Logan's an astute man. He'll read you like you've got your social diary taped to your forehead. You could fit a whole year on a Post-It note.

She sat up, still stark naked, and noticed her watch lying on top of her shirt, on top of her underwear, on top of her jeans, all neatly folded on the ground next to one of the willow backrests. The man was resourceful, attractive and tidy, too. *Hooah.*

She loved the way he smiled at her when he ducked

back inside the tipi. He made her feel pretty. Inside, of course. Outside she was pretty ordinary. Quite sturdy. Typical Jane Wayne.

A lovely cross breeze made her nipples bead up. She lifted her hair off the back of her neck and closed her eyes. "Feels good."

She felt sexy. She kept her eyes closed and listened to him circle around her as though she were on display somewhere. She chose a museum. She was made of polished marble—sturdy, but far from ordinary. He opened and closed something. His paintbox, maybe, or his camera case.

"Lie back," he said as he knelt behind her. "This will feel even better."

She complied without cracking, smiled without cracking up. Wouldn't Mr. Wolf Track just howl if he could see inside her head? He poured water from a gallon milk jug into an enamel basin he'd placed above her head, dipped a natural brown sponge into it and smoothed it over her face and neck.

"You left your cap in the pickup, paleface. Your cheeks are pink."

"I forgot sunscreen. I'm not a good tanner." The water trickled into her hair, and she inhaled deeply. "Mmm, that tingles. It smells minty."

"Wild mint."

"It's lovely. I could take a bath in this."

"You are." He squeezed a stream of water from her throat through the valley between her breasts to her navel where he emptied the sponge and made her giggle. "Unlike you, my grandmother was a good tanner. She made soft brain-tanned hides, perfect for beading. She was very traditional." He dipped the sponge into the water again and gently mopped her breasts. "I used to help her gather plants. Wild mint has many uses."

"Which grandmother?"

"The one who mostly raised me."

"What happened to your parents?"

"They were around."

Eyes still closed, she breathed deeply, savoring the mint, contemplating the roundabout nature of his answers. Her questions seemed simple. Maybe too simple, too pointed. Or maybe he was actually giving her more than she knew how to ask for.

"I make my own horse liniment," he told her as he moved his wet hand over her belly. "Good for people, too. I make fly spray. Medicinal teas. My grandmother was a healer." Slow, soothing, sensuous circles. "Are you okay here?"

Her eyes flew open.

He pressed gently. "Here."

"Yes, I'm…why?"

"Some horses seem to know what a person is feeling. Maybe they all do, but they let it pass because most people don't notice anyway." His smile chased a chill she hadn't known she was harboring. "Most people aren't like you."

"I'm just a little off my feed lately." An understatement was no lie. It was a piece of the truth. A shard. Two could play the roundabout game. "Adobe was telling me he could empathize."

"If we took the fence down and stepped aside, he'd take his leave in a heartbeat."

"I'm not fenced in." She reached to touch his angular face. "Being here, being with you is very... liberating."

"Then stay here. Be with me."

She stared at the tipi's apex, where fifteen heavy lodge poles crossed in perfect balance, each one solidly supporting the rest. "It's like we're in a time warp. Nothing can touch us. Except us."

"What's a time warp? Someplace where time doesn't control you?" He stretched out beside her, tucking his hands beneath the back of his neck. "We had that, you know. My people had life. Your people brought time, which didn't make a lot of sense to us. Still doesn't."

"It's a way to manage things."

"It's a fence."

"You have fences, Logan. You put them up yourself."

"I know. It seems like the only way to manage what's left, but in the end it's all a crock. All I can really manage is myself." He turned to her and braced himself up on his arm. "We're going to take Adobe out today."

"Let him go?"

"Let him live a little." He touched her cheek with one finger. "You need to live a little. You're all tied up in time. Thirty days, sixty days." He gave a lopsided smile. "Greenwich, Zulu. Daylight Savings—what the hell is that about? You actually believe you can save the daylight?"

She laughed. "You know, I actually took a time management class once. I thought it would untie me. I found out that I was already doing it all right." She rolled her eyes and flashed a smile. "You know what unties me? Animals. My dogs untie me."

"What do they charge? As much as you paid for that class?"

She growled and nipped Logan's propping arm. He yelped, and then he howled and scooped her into his arms, and they laughed together until their sides hurt.

"We have a ceremony for untying," he told her when they went quiet again.

"Does it involve stealing watches?"

He growled and nipped her shoulder.

"It's about dogs, then."

"It can be about any kind of offense. The offender offers horses to the family he's wronged. It can be anything, even a killing. If the offended party takes the horses, the offender is untied, and no one is to speak of the matter again."

"What if they walk away without the horses?"

"Then the matter is unsettled until the offer is acceptable. But because it's about living together and not acquiring property, a generous offer is known to everyone. As long as it's honest, it would rarely be rejected."

"Do you still do that?"

"Not so much. We're pretty civilized. We've got courts and jails and plenty of people who think they're lawyers."

"And police?"

"Oh, we've always had police. You've gotta have police no matter who you are. Every city, every village, every post has its badasses."

"So this wonderful oasis, this time warp, it's no different for you than it is for anyone else. It isn't real. You can take time off from real life, but eventually you have to get back to it."

He chuckled. "Taking time off from life. Boggles the Indian mind." He stroked her arm. "Life is real. *You are life.* Time is something you guys made up to control life. Yours and everybody else's. It's a fence, Mary."

"Before I met you, I was counting the days until I could go back…to my so-called life." She pressed her cheek against the back of his hand. "Now I'm counting how many I have left before I have to go back."

"Stop counting the days."

"I'll try." She sat up, hands poised over the basin. "May I?"

"Help yourself. What's mine is yours."

"Good. I want your body." She took the sponge in hand. "You done me good, Wolf Track. Now it's your turn. Turn over and put your face on the rack while I do you back."

Laughing, he complied. "I don't think you can do me that way, baby, but I haven't seen as much of the world as you have."

"You have your grandma, and I have my continuing education classes. I've taken two in therapeutic massage. I use it on my dogs. Mint water?"

"Pour it on."

She poured more than bracing mint water. She attended to him with gifted hands, pressing away tension he hadn't known was there, replacing it with the kind of affection he craved. It was an intimacy complementary to their coupling, attention shared by people who cared for each other even when they were separate. He'd known little of this kind of attention, and it touched him deeply. It surprised him to think he could get used to this. He would think about the consequences later.

For now he basked in the beauty of having her hands all over his back. He wouldn't take his jeans off but his feet were bare, and she tended them with "advanced" techniques. He was glad he'd finally sanded off some of his calluses.

It was early evening when they finally went outside. Adobe raised his head. *Oh, there you are.*

"Ready for a family outing?" Logan asked the mustang. He opened the pen enough to let two two-leggeds in, which meant that one fleet four-legged could easily fly past them and get out if he wanted to. But they had the horse's attention, and they were getting his *what next?* look. Logan handed Mary the halter and coiled lead rope. "We're gonna get us some grass."

"We're going to go for a walk?"

"Just like walkin' the dog."

"Not quite." She fingered the halter, sorting out the part that would slip over the ears from the loop that would take the loose ends. She knew how to make the knot. One quick demonstration, and the knack was hers. But she still had her doubts. "If he decides to take off, this will be useless."

"Have you ever had a horse run away with you when you were riding? If he decides to take off, all you can do is bail out or go along for the ride. No muscle in your body can match his." He took the coiled part of the gear from her and left the halter in her capable hands. "He's bigger than a dog, Mary."

"And he eats grass."

"That's right."

"If a dog decides to rip my face off—"

"Like I said, no tooth in your head can match his." He steered her in the right direction. The horse was waiting. "Like you did before, let him come to you. Take the lead with your body."

"I'm the lead mare," she remembered, and then she scowled. "What are you smiling about?"

"Thinking about when you let me come to you."

Ah, a smile. "And I matched you, didn't I."

"With every fiber in your body."

"A terrible comparison."

"I'm not comparing. I'm saying your body knows how to lead. Adobe gets it. I get it." He smiled back. "Now, you go, girl."

When they walked, the horse walked. When they stopped, he grazed. They sat in the grass, listened and watched. The sun had lost its unremitting power over the prairie for the day, and all that lived there enjoyed the soft light and easy warmth of its gentler side. From a sidehill a meadowlark tweedled in the grass. Another answered. A breeze lifted Mary's hair, and Logan drank in the simple beauty of her face. He saw it more and more, the kind of loveliness that made a man's throat sting.

"My sister likes you," he told her, because it was the best praise he could come up with. He could have told her that her profile against the early evening sky was a real grabber, but she wasn't one to take just any kind of praise to heart. "For one thing, she thinks you're some kind of hero. What you do saves lives."

"The dogs save lives." She draped her forearms

over upraised knees. "That's not why they're doing it, of course. They don't set out to save lives."

"How do you know?"

"They do it because the handler asks them to. They appreciate the hands that feed them."

"You have good instincts. You know how to ask. What you do saved my nephew's life. If you have to go back..." He'd allowed *if* to replace *when* in his thinking. "It's for a good cause."

"Mustang Sally's Makeover Challenge could be a lifesaver for these horses."

"Your father has petitioned the Bureau of Indian Affairs for a hearing about the leases." From his sister to her father. Hell of a leap, but there was some balance in there somewhere. He was beginning to know Mary's needs, and balance was a big one. "He has some powerful friends."

"You mean Senator Perry. They go way back."

"Which means your father has some pull with the Bureau of Land Management. Perry's on the Energy and Natural Resources Committee, which is sitting on a bill that would force the BLM to protect wild horses and burros instead of this half-assed *management* program they're pushing. They're calling it the ROAM Act."

She surprised him with a smile. *"Half-assed."*

"There's a group of women who've adopted burros, call themselves 'The Wild Ass Women.' That's my kind of woman."

"Really," she marveled.

"Oh, yeah. It's women who'll push for this ROAM Act. It was a woman who got the whole thing started. Called her Wild Horse Annie. Way back in the fifties she started the ball rolling by getting them to stop the aerial roundups for slaughter. They'd almost run the wild horse into extinction, along with the buffalo and yours truly."

"You weren't born yet."

"I don't mean just me. I'm not *just* me. And I'm more than bloodlines." He nodded toward the horse, who didn't give a rip about anything but ripping up a little grass. "So is he, but that's a whole different branch on the political tree. I'm talking rescue. You think it's men coming to the rescue, but it's—"

"I do?"

"That's the way they tell it, but I'm here to say it's more likely women. You and your dogs, for one. And we've got our own Mustang Sally." Adobe moved on to a new patch of grass, and Logan nodded, watching intently. "Mustang Sally. Don't slow down, baby. Don't ever slow down."

"You came to the rescue."

He looked at her curiously.

"If your former wife could leave two children with you, she probably would have left them without you. Did you adopt them before or after she left?"

"I didn't have time before she left." He glanced away. "Maybe I did. See how useless time is when you're having fun? It was the fun that ran out. Time was nothing, and life went on." He smiled at the hills. "To this very day."

"I'm not my father," she said quietly.

"You think we don't know that?"

"Who's *we?*" She gave a dry laugh. "The Tutan brand is pretty well known. Around here, anyway."

"Change it." It was her turn to shoot the curious look. He lifted one shoulder. "There are lots of ways to change it. You get married, you change it. You get divorced, you change it back. You get adopted…"

"Adopt me," she said cheerfully. "You do that, don't you? Adopt people into the tribe?"

"I did it through the state with the boys. All nice and legal, so they could have my name. But I can't adopt you into the tribe. Can't adopt my sons into the tribe. Some white guy says he was adopted into the Sioux Tribe, check his legs. One's bound to be longer than the other." He raised his brow. "It's all about blood."

"But what about all of us being related?"

He chuckled. "That would put a whole new spin on what we did earlier."

"Seems to me I heard that somewhere."

"*Mitakuye Oyasin.* All my relatives." He sat up. "Yeah, the blood quantum thing, that came from the U.S. government. We've gotta be enrolled. So I can adopt you our way, if that's what you want. But that doesn't make you a member of the 'vanishing race.'"

He glanced away. "Or, I can marry you and change your name your way."

"*My* way? Maybe I'd want to keep my name. Just change the Tutan brand."

"If anybody can do it, you can." He snapped his fingers. "Just like that, you won my sister over." He nodded toward the horse. "And him. You had him at…whatever your body told him."

"It wasn't—"

"Don't worry. I'm not jealous. I'm getting my own messages." He touched her shoulder on his way to standing up. "And I like them just fine."

"Where are we going?"

"That's up to the lead mare. Find us some greener grass."

Adobe went quietly into the round pen after they'd watered him at the creek. It felt good to watch him get his groove back. His world suited him perfectly. He could no longer live there, but it was a nice place to visit. Prize money notwithstanding, Logan's goal was to make Adobe's transition as agreeable as possible. Whoever won the bid on this horse would be getting a prize that had little to do with money. They would have a heroic creature, one that had come to his family's rescue. Whether he liked it or not.

It was the kind of summer evening the prairie saved up for. When the wind rested, the prairie broke out the fireflies and cranked up the crickets. The sun made a splash when it sank behind the buttes, spraying rosy streaks across the sky and putting up purple cloud drifts for good measure.

They roasted buffalo kabobs and marshmallows. The buffalo was crisp on the outside, rare on the inside, and the marshmallows were blackened. "Just the way I like 'em," Logan said. He hadn't roasted marshmallows since his sons were kids, and he'd never licked them from a woman's fingers. She said she'd never had her fingers licked by anyone without a tail. He added sage to the dying fire, and the pungent smoke kept the mosquitoes at bay.

He brought blankets outside, and they lay on their backs and got lost in a night sky overflowing with stars. As many diamonds on black velvet would have paled in comparison, but he would have found a way to offer them to this woman if such a gift would persuade her to stay with him. He'd asked her, but she hadn't taken him seriously. Or maybe she had and she'd pretended otherwise. But, no, she was no pretender. She had passed the four-legged test. Animals were like children. They could smell a fake a mile away.

"I should go," she said to the night sky.

"Where?"

"Back to…" She turned away from him and made ready to push up. "Back."

"Back to back." He reached for her and pulled her back down, her back flat against his chest. His arms encircled her. He slipped one hand under her shirt and cupped a bare breast. She drew a deep breath and filled his hand with soft flesh. He kissed the side of her neck.

She wasn't going anywhere.

"I vote for belly to belly," she said. "But I'm willing to compromise."

Chapter Eight

Mary awoke to bird chatter and man song.

The hills on the horizon were crimson, but the heart of the promise had yet to appear. *Come come come,* the birds chirped. The man's voice was less urgent, more evocative. She propped herself up on her elbows and scanned the shadows, but she saw no singers. They were all sound, and the sound felt sacred.

Mary threw off the blanket she'd shared with Logan and followed her first instinct. *Get up and go after the voice.* But within a few steps she saw the light and stopped dead in her tracks. The singer's pitch rose in concert with the sun's slow rising, and it struck her that this was not her moment. No one had summoned her. This was not a show. There would be no sermon. Her appearance was unwarranted. The emotion in Logan's voice was not for her, but it was a gift nonetheless, there for her to enjoy along with sunrise.

Adobe stood quietly, ears perked, soaking in the music and the morning. Once the sun had topped the horizon, the song sank into silence and Mary was drawn to the mustang. He would welcome water from the creek. Calmly and without hesitation Adobe stood for her haltering, followed where her shoulder led and stopped behind her on the bluff overlooking the creek. They both saw the nude man standing knee deep in the water below, but only one held her breath.

Good God, he was glorious.

Logan had his back to them, which gave Mary time to gather her wits and proceed carefully. Tumbling down the hill after Jack was fine for Jill, but Mary channeled Tuesday's child, full of grace. Logan glanced over his shoulder, and she bid him a high-pitched good morning. "That looks wonderful," she said too cheerily. "We might just try it ourselves."

"Not there. Too deep. Bean-shriveling cold, too." He grinned as he waded to the bank. "Maybe you noticed."

She managed to stifle the better part of a laugh. After that awe-inspiring backside, there was something else she was supposed to notice?

"Oh, so that's how it is. You come down this way and laugh, woman." He stepped out of the water, pulled a towel off a chokecherry bush and nodded in her direction as he took quick swipes at his arms and legs. "The current's stronger than it looks down there. I don't want it to take you away."

"Do you know how beautiful…" She started upstream, thoroughly captivated. Adobe hadn't had his water yet, but he went where Mary went, swishing his tail behind him. "What were you singing?"

"Oh, what a beautiful morning!" he sang, arms outstretched. He'd been in better tune in Lakota.

"So that's how it is," she teased, fascinated by the way he put on his jeans one leg at a time like everyone else. Except the people who started with underwear. "More code."

"No kidding, that's pretty much what I was singing. You've heard them sing their sunup song in the Middle East, right? Sunrise is the same in any language."

"It's prettier here."

"That's because this is home." He tipped his head to the side and smiled as Adobe ripped up a mouthful of big bluestem and tall switch grass. "It's our place."

"Rightfully so." She glanced across the creek, and there stood a clutch of Mexican redhat coneflowers ablaze in the slanted sunlight, their petals folded back at the base of long brown heads like…

Oh, for Pete's sake, Mary.

She grinned like a school girl suddenly seeing Freudian symbolism everywhere she looked. "It was a beautiful night, wasn't it? I've never seen such bright stars. Not even in the desert."

"Good company turns it all up a notch." He sat down in the grass to put on his boots and looked up at her, one eye squinted closed against the sun. "What date are we on?"

"On the calendar?"

"It's time I took you to a dance."

"Time?" She stepped back as Adobe stretched toward water. "Did you say *time?*"

"Wanna go to a powwow with me?" Logan pushed off the ground and grabbed his shirt from the cherry bush. "The *Hanskaska* celebration is tonight. Wolf Hide Bearers. It's an old warrior society."

"Are you a Wolf Hide Bearer?"

"I belong to *Tokala,* the Kit Fox Society, one of our *Akicita.* More for policing than soldiering."

"Like an MP?"

"But not military. You're soldier police. I'm camp police." He finished buttoning his shirt, started tucking it into his jeans. "What do you say? Have you been to a powwow?"

"I haven't. Isn't that awful? I grew up right down the road—" he joined in on *right down the road* and had her smiling "—and I haven't been to a powwow. Tonight?"

"Let's take our boy into town and see how he takes to a saddle. Maybe I'll put you on Hattie and we'll do a little riding." He reached for Mary's hand, and the three of them started up the hill. "And we'll stop by and say hello to your mother."

"You're a kind and gentle man, Wolf Track. I don't think I've ever dated a real gentleman before."

"Kind and gentle goes with the fox, not the wolf. I was born a wolf, but I learned to be a fox."

"The fox is sly," Mary pointed out.

"*Your* fox is sly. Ours is swift and clever, but also gentle. He lives close to the ground, so he knows a lot about plants that feed the soul and heal the body. One of our songs says, 'I am the fox. I am supposed to die. If there is anything difficult, anything dangerous, that is mine to do.'"

"Sounds like the words of a soldier."

"You understand what it means to police your own. A soldier must go all out in his fight, all teeth and claws. But when you police your own people, you can't lose the gentle side of your nature. It takes strength to be gentle."

"So your kind of fox wouldn't raid the henhouse," she said as she led Adobe toward the section of the round pen she'd left standing open.

"Ha! Are you kidding? All those lovely hens tended by one overworked cock?" Logan squeezed her hand. "They beg to be raided."

* * *

Audrey was happy to see her daughter and genuinely pleased to see her with Logan. She fussed over coffee, followed by ham and cheese omelets, followed by caramel rolls and more coffee. Logan knew when people liked him and when they were just blowing sunshine to get whatever they wanted out of him. Audrey wanted to keep her daughter around as long as possible, but she liked Logan. She approved of him. He could see it in her eyes. As long as no mention was made of her husband, Audrey was a cheerful soul. Logan noisily sucked cinnamon and sugar off his fingers, one at a time, as he savored another jolt of satisfaction over denying Damn Tootin the use of a beautiful chunk of Indian land.

"Need another napkin?" Audrey was already halfway out of her chair.

"No, no." Logan waved the notion away with his unsticky hand. "None of this should be wasted on paper. Mmm. My sister makes great pies, but otherwise…mmm. My sweet tooth just died and went to heaven."

"I wrapped up a whole fresh batch to take with you," Audrey said. "They're not on my diet, and Dan shouldn't be eating them, either." She set the heavenly-scented package on the table in front of Logan. "I love to bake caramel rolls. It brings me good luck. Sometimes out of the clear blue it brings me visitors."

"I'll bet you can smell them all the way out to the highway," Logan said. "Especially once you've tasted them. You can be sure they'll bring me back."

"Every Friday morning," Audrey said. "Like clockwork. You be here."

"Logan's a worker, but he isn't much for clocks."

Logan laughed. "For your mother's caramel rolls, I'll buy myself a damn watch with one of those perpetual calendars on it."

"Careful," Mary warned. "She might be in cahoots with the tooth fairy."

"That tooth is like a cat," he said. "Many lives. All it takes is a whiff of lovin' from something in the oven."

"You have my recipe, don't you, Mary?" Audrey reached across the table and patted her daughter's hand.

"I've never seen a recipe," Mary said.

"It's in my head. Heart." The woman smiled at Logan, eyes a-twinkle. "I know it by heart, but I can write it down for you."

The road to Sinte was busier than usual, and the rhythm of the dance drum was the cause. "Wait 'til dusk," Logan said. "The only time of the year we get bumper-to-bumper traffic. Except for funerals, but those aren't seasonal."

"We're coming back then, aren't we?"

"Well, yeah. We've got a date."

They drove past the gate to the powwow grounds on their way to his place. He flashed her a smile, pleased that she was looking forward to the celebration. He was looking forward to it, too—feeding her Indian tacos and maybe a snow cone, trying to trick her into sampling some *taniga*—traditional tripe. Soldiers were generally pretty adventuresome eaters.

Adobe unloaded as sweet as a trail horse. Logan put him in with Hattie, and they got reacquainted while Mary helped him haul out the saddles. She insisted on doing her share, and he wasn't one to argue. The mustang accepted the saddle blanket after a couple of tries, but be damned if he was willing to take on a heavy saddle.

"Let me ride him bareback."

"I wasn't gonna let you ride him at all."

"Just let me try." She tapped her forehead with the heel of her hand. "What am I saying? *Let me.* We're equal partners here, and I know he'll let me ride him."

"How good are you bareback?"

"We'll see. We won't be going far, will we? If he balks, I'll walk back. But he won't do that, will you, 'Dobie'?"

"Don't push it, okay?"

She didn't have to. It was a rough ride for her, but only because Adobe didn't know how to carry a rider. By the end of the ride to the end of his pasture and back—about two miles—the horse had gone through all his gaits, and Mary had stuck with him. She bobbled and bounced around, but, damn, she had guts, grit and great legs.

They met Hank and Sally at the powwow grounds. Sally was using her cane, and Hank carried a folding three-legged stool on a stick. Seating could be hard to come by at a summer powwow, and Sally thrived on the freedom to come and go as she pleased. For her part, Mary was all eyes, ears and nose. The smell of meat and wood smoke, yeasty dough fried in lard and strong coffee, pine pitch and trampled grass and summer dust mingled with laughing adults and squealing children, the swish of long leather fringe on beaded traditional dresses, the tinkle of hundreds of tiny metal cones dangling from a jingle dress, and the rustle of feathers. The colors were glorious. Some of the fancy dancers could easily have been mistaken for exotic birds as they strutted about the grounds like cocks of the walk.

The heart of the powwow grounds was the bowery—a huge circle of plank benches sheltered by a leafy thatch of cottonwood branches to form an arena with a flagpole in the middle. There was an announcer's stand, yard lights, half a dozen drum groups scattered around the perimeter and a grass dance floor open to the night sky. The children's contests had been held during the day, followed by the women, who were finishing up with the last round of shawl dancing as the men gathered outside the bowery.

"Why aren't you dancing tonight?" Hank asked Logan.

"You sing, I'll dance."

Hank laughed. "You got me there."

"You can't compete when you're on the committee, and they've always got me on the committee. Besides, I have a date." A slow cadence on the drum prompted him to take Mary's hand. "*Kahomni*. Come on, this is intertribal."

"Intertribal?" she asked.

"Any tribe. Even yours." He pulled her into a growing boy-girl-boy-girl circle, people in and out of costume. "Intertribal means no contest, and *Kahomni* is the Rabbit Dance. It's our two-step."

The dancers held hands. The step was uncomplicated, and the rhythm matched a lover's heartbeat, steady and resolute. Mary's palms felt clammy. She glanced up at Logan, who winked at her and squeezed her hand. She was thoroughly charmed, even felt a little dizzy with it. A little discombobulated. Men didn't wink at her. She wasn't easily charmed.

And she almost waited too long to excuse herself and head for the bathroom.

Mary waited in line for a turn at the blue biffy. Something was either very wrong or very right. She felt vaguely crampy, which should have been welcome at long last. But it seemed strangely forbidding, like every other weird turn her body had taken on her lately. She couldn't abide the possibility of being pregnant now, but if she *was* pregnant, and then she wasn't…that thought scared her almost as much as the other. What the hell was wrong with her head?

Probably nothing. Somewhere along the line she'd given common sense a furlough.

Okay, it was her turn to use the head. Latrine.

She wasn't sure she wanted to close the door all the way. Close, rank smelling quarters didn't do her stomach any good, but the anxious faces peering back at her settled the question of closing the door. She'd certainly had less privacy in cruder facilities, but her pulse was pounding like machine gun fire, and she wanted to bolt. Not much light, not enough air, couldn't tell much of anything. If there was blood, it was minimal. The beginning of something, the end of something—only God knew. And He wasn't picking a place like this to answer any stupid questions.

Mary took a detour into a copse of trees, found a place to sit, put her head down to stave off a wave of dizziness. She used her shirttail to wipe cold sweat off her face. She'd half thought about talking to her mother. She'd half thought about talking to Sally. Half thoughts were easily abandoned. As long as they weren't fully formed, Mary could still get away. Go back to Fort Hood, back to work, get busy and figure things out. She had plenty of options, *good* options, readily available to her where she really wanted to be, where everybody knew her name because it was pinned to her uniform.

All she'd needed was a little fresh air and she was ready for Act Two. She rejoined the group just as Sally was saying to Logan, "Be there or be square, and you know I can't be square. Not even on a dare." Seated beside Hank at the end of a plank bench, she looked up at Mary.

"Who would dare?" Mary meant to smile, but she couldn't quite pull it off.

"Well, that's just it. And that's..." Sally turned back to Logan. "...why I'll be there. Moral support. Right, Hank?"

"I dare you to stay home and let Logan handle him," Hank ventured. "A move that *would be* just it."

"Why do I feel like somebody just said, 'Shh. Here comes Mary'? If you're planning a raid on the Tutan lands, I like chicken, too."

"I wish," Logan said. "It's just a meeting."

"The hearing my father wants?" Mary tucked her arm around Logan's—a little affection, a lot of support. "Listen, I'm on your side. Don't treat me like the big white elephant in the room."

"It's a *meeting*. And if you were an elephant, we couldn't fit you in with the eight hundred pound gorilla." His grin faded. He looked at her closely. "You okay?"

Mary pressed her lips together and nodded.

Sally missed the exchange. "Hey, that friend of yours is interested in the competition. The guy from Wyoming."

"Dane? You found him?"

"You can find anyone on the Internet. He thinks pretty highly of you. Can you think of anyone else?"

"Not off hand, but I'll…" Mary frowned as she looked up at Logan. "The land should go to the horses. How can my father have any say in the matter? When is this meeting? It might mean something if I'm on your side." Still hanging onto Logan's arm she gave a little smile. "I'm the eight hundred pound gorilla's white elephant daughter."

"Hard to ignore a pair like that." He returned her smile. "But Indian politics is no different from any other kind. Thorny as hell, and I've got the scars to prove it. When the Bureau of Indian Affairs sticks its nose into it because there's land involved, somebody from Washington might try to pull something on us. Helping out a friend."

"And I know just…," A sharp cramp deep in her belly took Mary's breath away.

Logan put his arm around her. "What's wrong?"

"I just need to sit down for a minute."

"Sit here." Hank stood quickly. "How about some water?"

"I think…I think I should go. I should lie down."

She laid her cheek against Logan's shoulder. "I'm sorry."

"We'll get you to my house," he said gently.

"Need any help?" Hank asked.

"No, thanks. It'll go away. All I need is ..." She glanced at Sally and rolled her eyes, woman to woman. "Better timing."

Logan wasted no time hustling her through the maze of vehicles in the tamped-grass parking lot. The knot in Mary's stomach twisted tighter as the pickup bumped over the rutted entrance road. At the gate they would turn onto the blacktop—right for Logan's place, left for Sinte.

"Do you think they'd see me at the Indian hospital?"

He gave her a cut-the-crap look. "What is it?"

"An emergency." She gave her head a tight shake. "Or not. But say it is, they wouldn't turn me away, would they?"

He gunned the engine and arced the steering wheel hard left. "Two minutes."

Logan waited in the hallway outside the emergency exam room. He wasn't one to speculate about another person's business, but he cared for this woman. It shook him deeply to see her in pain. He'd thought she was in better shape than he was, and he was pretty damn fit. He tried to remember everything they'd eaten—maybe she didn't have an iron gut like his, or maybe she'd eaten something this morning that had been left over from last night. That must've been it, and that was as far as his speculation was going. It wasn't anything bad. He thought about the mustang, the way he'd stood quietly with his head belly-level and he quickly dismissed the notion of a disease-detecting horse. Empathetic, sure, but horses didn't sniff out trouble the way dogs did.

And if it was a woman thing, that was definitely her business. A woman's body was to be respected, and a man, well, certain times he just steered clear. He was no match for a woman's life-giving power.

Which was why he was glad the doctor on call was a woman. His grandmother would have approved. But she would have instructed him to stop by on the way home and pick up some of her medicine.

"The pain has subsided," Dr. McKenzie told Logan when she finally emerged from the room. "I think it's going to be okay, but it's one of those wait-and-see situations. I offered to keep her overnight. It's up to her."

"What's going on?"

She nodded toward the room marked *Emergency*. "Go on in. She wants to see you."

Mary lay in a white room on a white table, her legs propped up and covered with a white sheet. Thank God she was able to turn her head when he walked in.

"Well, this is a fine mess." She offered a token smile. "I'm pregnant."

Logan stopped in his tracks. "That quick?"

She turned away and stared at an overhead light fixture. "Let's see if I've gotten the hang of this Indian humor. It looks like somebody beat you to the henhouse."

Dumbfounded, he took a step closer. Her light brown hair fell away from her ashen face and pooled beneath her head like an earthen pillow, and all he could think about was the way she'd looked lying on the ground beneath him and how badly he'd wanted to pour everything he was into everything she was. *That quick, that slow, that quick again.*

"You're not *that* swift and clever." She closed her eyes and sighed. "I'm sorry, Logan. I'm about six weeks along."

"And I put you up there on that mustang?" He passed his hand over his forehead. "Jeez. Why didn't you say something?"

"I was hoping the signs would go away." Gripping the sheet in both hands at her waist, she turned her face to him again, her eyes filled with a new sheen. "And you didn't put me up there. I put myself up there. So what does that say?"

He shook his head. "Do you feel okay?"

"What a beautiful man you are." Blinking furiously, she trapped her lower lip to stop it from trembling.

She was killing him. He wanted to kiss her, but he'd already made an ass of himself. *That quick.* What was he, twelve? He shoved his hands into the front pockets of his jeans.

She drew a slow, tremulous breath and found a way to smile. Not much, but for real. For him.

"I feel much better." She nodded, as if to punctuate her claim. "The cramping and, you know, everything else has stopped. It wasn't much. Just enough to wake me up. I wanted it to go away, and it almost did."

"What do you want now?"

She took a moment, as though the question of her wanting was totally unexplored. Then she levered herself up on her elbows and swung her legs over the side of the tall bed. He watched for a sign, a signal, a need he might meet. She offered none.

"I'd like to go someplace quiet and be still for a while." Hands on the edge of the bed, she steadied herself as though she were preparing to slide into a cold pool. "A hotel, I think, if you wouldn't mind taking me. The doctor said I should keep my feet up for a while."

"What about…"

"The father? There isn't one."

"I was gonna say your mother."

"She's with my father." She gave a dry chuckle. "Another father who isn't one."

"There's a father somewhere in this equation." He

wasn't going to ask. Damn him, he was not going to... "The guy you contacted about the competition?"

She shook her head. "The guy who dropped off a bunch of sperm on his way home from Iraq. Really. One time, one condom malfunction. That's all it takes." She snapped her fingers. "That quick."

"You can stay at my place." He sounded gruff, which was the way he wanted to be right now, the way he wanted to feel. "I can stay or go. It doesn't matter, either way."

"It matters to me." She touched the back of his hand. "You matter to me. I'm sorry. I really am."

"For what?" That hand was staying wedged in his pocket. "It's early, right? A few weeks. You didn't know."

"And, of course, no one else knows."

He looked her in the eye. His brain framed a stupid, stupid question. He clenched his jaw. *None of your damn business, Wolf Track. Keep your hands and your questions to yourself.*

Like that could happen the way he felt right now.

"You still want it to go away?"

"Oh, my God." She repeated the words until he took her in his arms, pressed her head to his chest and took her tears onto his shirt. "I'm scared. Why am I scared? Women have babies every day."

He couldn't speak. There was nothing he could

say. He was in love with her, and she was six weeks pregnant with somebody else's kid.

He was in love with her. Since when? Damn his hungry heart. With all the women out there, why pick this one? She looked up at him, smiling apologetically through tears he wanted to take away, and the word *why* took flight on its wings and tail. He felt the way he felt. He could either make an ass of himself and act on it, or he could do the decent thing and no more. Be a fool, or be, what? A gentleman?

What in holy hell was a gentleman?

"Today isn't your day," he said. "What do you want to do?"

"Stay at your place tonight." She looked up at him, her blue eyes awash. "If you don't mind."

"If I minded, I wouldn't offer. I'll wait for you at the nurse's station."

"This is my room." Logan stood tall in the middle of his short, nearly dark hallway and gestured left, and then right. "This is the spare room. Take either one."

"Is this a test?"

If it was, she wanted desperately to pass, at least the multiple choice portion. She'd already failed on filling in the blank. Whatever he thought of her at this point, it couldn't be good.

"No, and it's not a game. I'm in no mood for either one." He stepped closer, plunging his hands into his pockets again. He'd turned only one light on in passing, and it cast soft light and deep shadow over his chiseled face. "What are you afraid of, Mary?" His tone was as soft as the light. "You said you were scared. I'm just asking."

She was doomed to fail this one. She wasn't supposed to be afraid. She'd spent her adult life building herself up, body, mind and will. Her guard had been ironclad.

"I had everything under control. All regimented. My life on my terms."

"In a war zone?"

"That's the best place to learn to put your own house in order and keep it that way. You don't let yourself get emotional. Don't get buzzed up on anything that might take your guard down." She glanced left and right. *Which way?* "It was just stupid is all. It was careless and stupid and not even... He was going one way, I was going another, and our paths crossed."

"Did he hurt you?"

"Not...no." Oh, God, she looked weak. A horse with a broken leg. A dog with a broken leg could be dangerous. Couldn't she be that? A snarling bitch? One look into his gentle eyes cast that particular wish to the wind. "I hurt myself. I guess that's what scares me. I did this." She shook her head. "And I don't know what to do next."

"Pick a room."

Not what she'd expected, which was exactly what she kept telling herself she didn't want.

He nodded toward the door to the spare room. "That one doesn't get used much, and the bed sags in the middle." The other door drew a gesture. "This has a good bed, but it's full of my stuff."

"The bed?"

"The room. The bed's probably full of my smell, but I'll change the sheets for you."

She stared at the door to his room. "May I have your bed with you in it?"

"Not tonight."

"Then leave the sheets. I'll take what I can get."

Chapter Nine

Logan tapped on the door before he opened it. It was a warning, not a request. The woman was in his house, his room, his bed and he had something she needed. He left the door open, letting in the light from the hall. She moved to one side of the bed—*his* side on the rare occasions he'd shared. He preferred to be the caller rather than the called upon. Easier for the caller to call the shots. The called upon could hardly clear out, even when the call was clearly over.

He sat in the space she'd made for him. "Can you sit up a little? I made you some tea."

She braced herself up on her elbows and gave him the look that would have had a lesser man trying to remember which was his rifle and which was his gun.

Man, she had it down. But Logan was no raw recruit. His raw places had hardened over, and he knew how to fight and how to have fun.

He had to laugh. "You got a helluva nerve taking my bed. Maybe it was a test."

"If I minded, I wouldn't offer," she mimicked as she got herself situated, her back to the wall.

He handed her a mug and watched her take a sniff of the steam. "I didn't say I minded."

"What is this?"

"Mostly black haw root. It doesn't grow this far north, but I've got connections." He lifted one shoulder. "Well, I've got sisters. This is women's medicine."

"Men don't mess with it?"

"Men don't need it, and they don't share their bed with women who do." He chuckled. "But what the hell, I love a woman with nerve."

"In my case it wasn't easy to come by." She sipped noisily, raised her brow and sipped again. "Don't tell anyone I said I was scared," she whispered without looking up.

"You weren't scared to ride a wild horse."

"If I'd known I was pregnant, it would have been an irresponsible thing for me to do. I don't *do* irresponsible. That's not me." She rested the mug on her belly and the back of her head against the wall. She was still wearing her T-shirt, but he imagined bare legs beneath the bed sheet. She could not know how young and vulnerable she looked in the soft shadows.

Or maybe she did. The way she sighed seemed to say so.

"I know, I know," she said. "You pay your money, you go to the little girls' room, you take your big girl test. But that's only if you think you could possibly be pregnant." She rolled her head back and forth, seesawing with the wall as her fulcrum. "By some happy-to-get-lucky GI you hardly knew."

"The army could track him down for you." *But don't ask them to.*

"I could go get one of my dogs and track him down myself. Or, hey! How much wolf could a Wolf Track track?"

He smiled. "I don't care how much wolf he is. My only question is, dead or alive?"

"What a beautiful man you are," she whispered. "I don't want him tracked down. It was something that never should have happened. Believe it or not, something I don't do." She closed her eyes. "I mean…"

It occurred to him to ask *Believe which part? You don't want him back, or you don't…do?* But he wanted to be what she'd called him twice now—a beautiful man. Unselfish, uncritical—a simple *c'est la vie* kind of a guy.

"I wonder how Adobe knew," he said, and not just for something to say. He'd been privy to something pretty wonderful, and he'd wondered about it a lot.

"Some kind of vibration? Does he hear something or smell something? Is there some kind of gut feeling that only a guy with a huge gut can tap into?"

"You know how crazy that sounds?"

"To you? It doesn't sound crazy to you at all. You were willing to ride him."

"But I didn't know," she insisted. "I mean, I wasn't sure. I wasn't trying to…"

"Like I said, you've got a lotta nerve. You trusted the horse. What didn't seem possible to you was obvious to him, so you let him carry it for a while." An amazing conclusion, and he was pretty proud of himself for reaching it. Women and horses were wondrous creatures.

"Now that *does* sound crazy." She raised her cup in toast. "But I'm trusting you. I don't know what's in this cup, and I'm drinking it like it came in a teabag."

"How do you know what's in a teabag?"

"I know you wouldn't give me anything you wouldn't drink yourself."

"Yeah, I would. That's *women's* medicine." But he took the cup from her, sipped it noisily, grimaced comically. "Mmm. Yummy," he said, falsetto. He liked hearing her laugh. *She should be made to laugh often, and by someone who knows how.* He smiled, pleased with his version of an ad he'd seen on TV for an old movie he'd probably never see. "You ask me, men should do the heavy lifting for their pregnant women and keep their opinions to themselves."

He gave her back the cup, stretched out beside her and tucked his hands behind his head. "What scares you, Mary?"

"Babies."

"I've seen you with kids. You weren't scared."

"Their mother was close by."

"Their grandma. She's raised her share of kids, all but the first one. One of our grandmas raised him. He turned out pretty good." So had Logan, raised mostly by his grandma. There had been times, growing up, when some teacher or social worker had made it sound like they'd pitied his circumstances. It hadn't been easy, but he'd always managed to throw off the urge to tell them where to stuff it. They just didn't know any better.

"Is it the single parent part that scares you, or the fatherless kid?" he asked.

"Don't they add up to the same fear?"

"Nope. My former wife didn't want to be a single parent. She wasn't too worried about fatherless kids."

She touched his hair. "Not after she found you."

"I found her." She'd worked at the PX in the cosmetic department. She'd sold him some rank aftershave, said it reminded her of the ocean. He chuckled. "I was like Adobe. I was away from home, needed a family, and I found a woman with two kids and no man. The woman was hot, and the boys were really cool, and I was ready, willing and able."

"I can't imagine running away like she did."

"Can't you?"

"You thought she'd come back," Mary said quietly.

Ah, women. They had a way of burrowing under a guy's skin, rooting around for rhymes and reasons.

"Yeah, maybe. At first I did, sure. I figured we'd try again. But, hell, you can't hold your breath while you're taking care of two kids. Figured that out pretty damn quick."

"Funny you didn't get married again."

"Funny you're scared of babies."

She groaned. "With you it's *been there, done that*. With me it's *never been there, what if I can't do that*. Babies are small, and they need…"

"They start out small, but they grow on you." He grinned. "Well, first they grow *in* you, and then they grow on you."

"Easy for you to say."

"I know." He chuckled. "Men get off easy."

"You didn't. You bit off a big chunk of *never been there* and you did fine with it. The thing is…"

She went quiet for a moment, digging around for her own rhymes and reasons. It was the kind of pickax work he couldn't help her with. But he'd wait for whatever *the thing* was. He'd let her lay it on him.

"I don't need a family," she said softly. "I'm afraid I wouldn't be good at it."

Well, damn. Was this a red flag or a red herring?

"You're a good partner," he allowed, hoping it helped. "Better than I expected."

"What did you expect?"

"Nothing too complicated. I expected to be your teacher and the horse's trainer. I expected you to be able to ride the horse by the time we were through. I expected to win the competition."

"Two down and one to go."

"You're a full partner. I'm learning from you. Between you and Adobe, I'm seeing things I've never seen before. 'If wishes were horses,' you said. I have wishes, too."

"If we win, the money's yours." She touched his hair again, and his scalp tingled.

"I like your hands, Mary." He took hold of the one that was only flirting with the idea of actually touching his skin, and he rubbed it against his cheek. "The way you use them to greet the mustang, make him feel safe with you."

"I feel that way just watching your hands. I've never had much confidence in any hands other than my own."

He tipped his chin up for a glimpse of her. "You open all your own jars?"

"What jars?"

They smiled each other into a thoughtful silence. There were things he knew about this woman now, things she didn't seem to know about herself. He'd lived, and he'd learned. Maybe his gut wasn't as big as Adobe's. His senses were only human. But he knew Mary's heart, cloistered as it was within her strong body. She reminded him of his sons and his horses. None of them lied to him.

"Are you going back?" he asked.

"I have to go." She drew her hand away and raised the cup to her lips with both hands. She drank deeply, and then hurtled herself into explaining, "I have an important job to do. I made a commitment, and I don't renege on my commitments. And it's all I have." She laughed. *"All I have?* As Sally would say, that sounds so Hollywood. So *Jane Wayne."*

"Stay with me."

Silence dropped over them like a heavy wool blanket. Logan held his breath for fear of scaring her away. He could hear her heart racing. Or was it his? Both, he told himself. Two hearts racing toward a life together. Two people who didn't renege on their commitments.

One guy getting way the hell ahead of himself.

Lighten up.

"I'm no John Wayne, but I'll be your Tarzan. I'll help you raise Boy. Or Girl. I don't know much about girls, but between the two of us—"

"Are you serious?"

"If I wasn't serious, I wouldn't offer."

"What happened to *been there, done that?*"

"Those were your words, not mine." They didn't make much sense to him and didn't seem worth discussing. "This is what I have, this house and the half-section it sits on. Plenty of room for you to train your dogs, if that's something you want to keep doing. Keep an eye on your mother, who's *right down the road.*" He sat up, swung his legs over the side of the bed and turned to her. "You've more than delivered on your commitment. You don't have to stay in the army, Mary."

"I don't know that that's my main concern. We have pregnant soldiers, you know."

He kept his mouth shut and nodded.

"You don't get deployed while you're pregnant," she pointed out.

"But after the baby's born…"

"I could be sent anywhere." She shrugged. "Or I could file for a Chapter 8 discharge. Perfectly honorable, but not what I'd planned." She gave a dry laugh. "Planned parenthood is what I'd planned."

"Is it on your calendar?"

"What's on my calendar every month is an *E* for expected and a *B* for began. I'm short one *B*. It's not that I don't want to be a mother…*ever.* It's just that…" She sighed and flopped the back of her hand on the bed. "Okay, not like this. It wouldn't be right. And I'm not looking for a man to make things right."

"Because that wouldn't be right, either."

"Of course not. I have to make things right. You've already been a father to somebody else's…" she glanced at him and ventured "…children."

"And that's definitely not right."

"I don't mean that. It wouldn't be right to leave a baby…" She was wielding that pickax again, but this time she was digging at him. "See, your sons weren't *babies*. And you adopted them. And you were married to their mother."

"You're not supposed to reveal your code," he said. She screwed up her face, questioning his throw out of left field. "Your *B* and *E* thing. See, that's one of the differences between us. You keep the code to yourself, you can put your calendar anywhere you want. A man would never guess what that means."

"Or care."

"Marry me. I can be your child's father."

She stared at him as though he'd grown donkey ears.

He shrugged. "Or don't marry me. I can still be the father."

She looked in her cup. "What is *in* this stuff?"

"Roots."

She laughed a little too hysterically for his comfort.

"I want to be your husband, Mary. I'm not talking right or wrong here. I'm talking you and me. I'm *thinking* about you and me. I'm thinking we're good together." He stood slowly. "So, you think about it."

"You're feeling sorry for me, aren't you."

"Absolutely not. But you keep looking at me that way, you'll have me feeling sorry for myself pretty damn quick." He nodded toward the cup in her hand. "Is that helping any?"

"How is it supposed to help?"

"How the hell should I know? I told you, it's women's medicine. It's supposed to fix whatever's going on in those mysterious parts of yours. The parts I don't have." He cast a glance at the ceiling. "The parts I've been to and done, maybe, I don't know."

"Well, isn't that special?"

"You know what?" He pulled his gaze back down to earth, to the guarded look in her eyes. "I take it back. I take my offer back. I take my proposal back."

She shoved the mug at him. "Take your roots back."

"I take my roots back." He accepted the cup dispassionately.

"And take your bed back."

"You keep the bed. You've already…"

"Contaminated it?"

"Yeah. Exactly. *Contaminated it.*" He headed for the door. Clean exit, he told himself. No speeding, no slamming, no stomping. No stopping, Wolf Track. No looking back.

Damn.

"I'll be across the hall if...if you need any-thing."

She was laughing at him. And then she mumbled something about a man, and he felt like an idiot. Would it have helped if he'd gotten down on one knee?

He was a Lakota man, for God's sake.

"You're a beautiful man," she said under her breath when the words could not be heard unless they es-caped under the bedroom door.

And what I need is for you to touch me and keep touching me and don't stop touching me with the hands you use every day to fix things.

The deep, soft sound of men's voices pulled Mary to the outer edge of sleep.

Being surrounded by men's voices was nothing new for her, but being drawn from night into day by one voice in particular with such an exquisite sense of connection was a first. No man had ever found his way into her life so thoroughly—outside in and inside out—as Logan had done. He surely hadn't meant to, couldn't possibly know the depth of his incursion, but this morning Mary knew something new. She could tell by the way the sound of his voice lifted her that he had become part of her, and it had nothing to do with sex, nothing to do with genetic material. She'd made a lasting connection with a beautiful man, and no one could take that from her. Not even the man himself.

She put her jeans on, followed by socks and boots. She found a hairbrush on the dresser and took great pleasure in contaminating it with her hair. She wanted to leave a few strands behind. He wouldn't see them right away, but in a few weeks he'd notice and he'd miss her a little. She liked that idea.

She would miss him more than a little.

The unfamiliar voice belonged to another fine-looking man in a cowboy hat. He wasn't as tall as his younger brother, and his face was more refined. He was clearly at home in Logan's kitchen, and the look he gave Mary when she walked in was easy, friendly, maybe pleasantly surprised.

"Mary, this is my older son, Trace." Arms folded, the two men stood side by side like bookends for the coffee fixings on the counter behind them. Trace touched the brim of his hat. He'd been raised a cowboy. "He's the real rider in the family. Only he likes his ride as wild it gets."

"You're the bronc rider." Mary pulled out a chair and sat down at the table. She wasn't feeling up to elbowing anyone aside at the coffee station.

"And you are the…"

"Logan and I teamed up for Mustang Sally's Wild Horse Makeover."

"Wow. You get to train a horse with Logan Wolf

Track?" Trace gave Logan a mock once-over. "I don't see a cast on you anywhere."

"I don't mind working with somebody, as long as she's interested. You know that." Logan opened a pine cupboard door and took out a mug. "Coffee or tea, Mary?"

"Whatever's easy."

"Same as before?" Without waiting for an answer, he reached back into the cupboard and pulled out a plastic bag. "Mary's a fine partner," he told Trace, who was more interested in the plastic bag than Mary's attributes. "That horse took to her right off."

"The *horse* did?" Trace scowled. "What the hell are you smoking now?"

"It's not for you, so don't worry about it." Logan filled a small saucepan from the tap and put it on the stove.

Trace turned the burner on for him. "Just making sure. I don't want them haulin' my dad in front of some cable TV camera asking him if he inhaled." Logan gave him a look, and Trace grinned. "You wouldn't think he'd be old enough to be my father, would you, Mary?"

"Older brother, maybe."

"See, Logan? I'm even starting to look like you. And you look damn good for an old man."

"You don't have to sell me to her, Trace. She's checked my teeth."

"They're all there, right?" Trace asked Mary. "I'm here to tell you, there's nothing false about this man."

"He's about to hit me up for something." Logan made a *gimme* gesture. "Let's have it. Anything but the keys to the pickup."

"You've got me confused with my brother." Trace pulled the glass pot from the coffee maker. "I saw Ethan a few weeks ago. He's doing okay." He offered Logan first refill.

Logan nodded. "I saw him the other day. He was entering up in the competition."

"Against you?" Trace chuckled as he poured. "Glutton for punishment, that guy."

"Not from me. I've never been keen on punishment."

"He used to tell me, you'll catch more flies with honey," Trace told Mary. "And I couldn't figure out what he was gonna do with all those flies." He glanced at Logan. "Is Ethan still around?"

"I ran into him at the Drexlers' place. He hasn't come around here."

"He will." Trace sipped his coffee, and then he gestured toward the window above the sink. "You've got a great looking horse out there. You want me to buck him out for you?"

"He's kidding," Logan assured Mary. "He knows better."

Trace shrugged, making a face as he watched

Logan sprinkle dried brown bits into the saucepan. "He might make a good calf horse. I just finished one out for a guy who can't rope worth beans, but that horse will make him look good right up until he throws his loop away."

"Sign up and get your own horse," Logan said.

"Sally's looking for more competitors," Mary said. "Somebody like you could attract some publicity for the cause."

"Three Wolf Tracks would definitely be a crowd. I'm gonna cook you some breakfast, Mary. How are we fixed for eggs?" Trace stuck his head behind the refrigerator door and called out, "Damn, Logan, how do you survive?"

"There's bacon in there," Logan said.

"Yeah, but that's about it." Trace closed the door and caught his dad's eye.

"The bacon's all we got shakin'," the two men said in unison, both grinning.

Trace shook his head. "I'm gonna have to sign you up for Meals On Wheels just to make sure you get a balanced diet."

"Mary knows all about 'meals on wheels'," Logan said. "She's done a couple of tours in Iraq."

"That's what we call the MKT. Mobile kitchen trailer." She smiled. "Meals on wheels."

"You're in the army *now?*" Trace hummed the tune to his question, and Mary nodded. "What did you do? Go over the hill?" he teased.

Logan shoved Trace's shoulder. "She's on leave."

"Look at this guy, coming to your defense. You can just tell he's—"

"About to pour honey down your throat, boy." Logan set Mary's tea in front of her and joined her at the table.

"Otherwise he'd be the one joshin' you," Trace said.

"I've been thoroughly joshed," she said into her cup before she took her first sip.

Logan dropped his face into his hand.

"Time out." Grinning, Trace clapped a hand on his father's shoulder. "No more joshin' on an empty stomach. How about I make an egg run?" He used his hand as a stop sign. "Don't say it. I called time out."

"You cooking?"

"Oh, yeah." Trace laughed. "Logan's good at a lotta things, but cooking ain't one of 'em."

Trace took his coffee with him along with Logan's order for butter and juice. He left them sitting kitty-corner from each other in awkward silence.

"I'm sorry about last night," Mary said at long last.

"Forget about last night."

She nodded and concentrated on her tea. *Take your medicine like a good soldier.* She wondered how Trace and Ethan had been encouraged to take their medicine. Cowboy up? Be brave?

Growing up, she'd certainly never been encouraged to be a good soldier. She'd helped in the kitchen, but she'd never really done any cooking. Her mother had encouraged her to do her homework, but only after the chores were done. And she didn't want to run into her father while she was doing her chores because he'd have a few more for her to do. She was going to have to take over someday now that her "worthless" brother had flown the coop. And cooped she was. The kind of banter Logan had traded with his son never happened in the Tutan household. Not when Father was around.

"If you feel up to it, we can do some ground work with Adobe this morning," Logan said. "Show him off to Trace. I have a meeting later."

"I should spend some time with my mother." She looked into his eyes, hoping for some sign that he didn't mean *forget completely*. It wasn't there. The warm smile she expected to find waiting for her in his dark eyes was not there. She glanced away. "And Sally. I should explain to Sally."

"They'll be able to help you out," he said. "Woman to woman."

"Is today's meeting the one with my father?"

"I can handle your father."

"I know, but just don't…" She laid her hand on his forearm. "He's had his way over that land long enough. It's time for a change."

Logan nodded.

"Just don't ever turn your back on him. Don't ever think he's given up."

"My business with your father is my people's business. It isn't personal. His time is over." He gave a perfunctory smile. "The *times* have changed."

She smiled back. "Which times, Wolf Track? Central? Mountain? Daylight savings?"

"All of the above." He tossed an invisible timepiece over his shoulder. "Out the window. Indian time rules here now, baby."

"Baby?"

"Hell, yeah. Killer-sweet. You gotta love 'em, even when—*especially* when they're breaking your heart." He slid his hand into her hair and met her halfway for a deep, demanding, unstinting, unhurried kiss. Then he rested his forehead against hers and whispered, "You'll see."

Chapter Ten

Mary loved her mother, and she missed her, but the woman she missed was not the timid soul who slipped quietly from room to room in the Tutan house like a sad specter. It was painful to see the mainstay of what was once her home fade into the woodwork of a mere house. Mary felt guilty about these thoughts, and her guilt made it doubly hard to come to her mother's kitchen for a heart-to-heart. They made tea, and they sat side by side on the big banquette in the sunny nook that housed the kitchen table—one of the few bright spots in the house—and neither of them spoke. Not right away.

"I had a checkup yesterday," Audrey said finally.

"Oh, God." Mary slapped her forehead. "Mother, I'm sorry. I was going to go with you."

"Your father dropped me off. There was someone he had to meet with anyway, so it worked out just fine."

Audrey laid her thin hands palms down on either side of Grandma's pink Depression glass salt and pepper shakers. The rings that had been Grandma Tutan's clicked against the table. The Tutan family rings, supposedly destined for Mary's hand someday since her brother had refused them. She wouldn't hurt her mother if she could help it, but...

It would be a cold day in hell before she would wear those rings. It was a hard thought, a mean thought.

"I got a good report."

Oh, God. Mary took her mother's hands and held on for dear life. Dear, dear life. Words so rarely said under the Tutan roof burned in her throat. Tears stung her eyes. All she could do was squeeze, nod and whisper, "Good...good, good."

When she was able to breathe easily again, she unclenched her hands and let herself lean until gravity brought her down, and Mother took her daughter's head in her lap.

"Did you think I was a goner?" Audrey asked. Mary closed her eyes and drifted in the timeless comfort of being stroked by a mother's hand. "Hmm?"

"I couldn't, no." *And I couldn't know.*

"I'm here," Audrey said. "So tell me what's bothering you. Maybe I can help you sort it out. Or just listen. Whatever you need."

"When did I become so transparent?"

"To me?" Audrey made a wistful sound. "When they cleaned you off and handed you to me. Your skin was like tissue paper, and you had a protective glaze over your face, as though you really had just come from an oven. I saw everything, every precious part."

"Since you know me so well, it would be comforting if this came as a surprise, okay?"

"Okay."

The frail hand continued to stroke Mary's hair.

"I'm pregnant."

Audrey drew a long, slow, deep breath. "Wow."

"Wow?"

"I'm surprised. Wow. You can tell that quickly?"

Mary sat up laughing. "That's not the reaction I was looking for, but any surprise will do."

"Well, I *am* surprised, but you know what you're doing. You know what you want. You'll be a wonderful mother." She smiled and touched her daughter's cheek. "I'm happy. Are you happy?"

"I don't know. I'm still surprised."

"How does Logan feel about it?"

"The truth is…" Hard to admit only because it was so far from what she wanted it to be.

"I can tell you how he feels about it." Dan Tutan strolled from the dining room shadows into the light, hands firmly planted on his ample hips. "Pretty damn proud of himself. Dan Tutan's daughter makes a nice little feather in his war bonnet."

Mary closed her eyes and fought for control, starting with her voice. Soft and steady. "I'm leaving, Mother. Would you like to go with me?"

"No, she would not. She's already had one heart attack. Are you trying to give her another one?"

Mary slid to her feet. "Mother?"

"I'm fine, Mary. I'll be right here." Audrey gave a subtle wave of her hands. "Don't get into it now. Go."

"You should come with me, Mother. You don't need this." Mary reached out, leaning into her plea. "Mother, I'm going to need help with this baby. Come with me."

"You'll have all the help you need. He's a wonderful man."

"Mother, it isn't..." She glanced at her father. *Glared* at her father. What it was and was not was none of his business. She would allow him no more—not another word, not another moment. *No more.* "I want you to call me, Mother. If anything happens, anything changes, I want to..." She swallowed against the needles in her throat. "He has no right to take you away from me."

"Nothing can take me away from you. I'm going

with you in ways you'll soon begin to understand."
Audrey smiled and nodded. "Go. Be happy."

Sally had always been easy to talk to. Bring her
your latest hardship and you were soon persuaded
to throw most of the heavy stuff overboard and go
with the flow. But Mary's news threw Sally, at least
enough to abruptly silence the front porch swing.

Wide-eyed, she leaned toward Mary. "How did
that happen?"

"Um…"

"You know what I mean. I knew you two would
hit it off, but what a—" She whooped, clapped her
hands together and brandished them right and left
victoriously.

"Don't say *bang*," Mary warned. She wanted to let
the fantasy live. Logan's baby. The more she thought
about it, the more she wished for it. It could have
been. It *should* have been. But she had to remember
that it was not. "Wrong word."

"So inappropriate." Sally grinned as she pushed
the ball of her sneaker against the porch floor with
one foot and got them swinging again. "I've seen you
two together. You were meant to be. And I ca-a-lled
it," she sang out.

"Seriously, Sally."

"Seriously, *Mary*." She nodded toward the big
white pickup parked in front of the house. "I'm

dying for details, but we have to get going. There's a meeting at the tribal office."

"Is it about the land?"

"I don't know those details, either. Committee meeting, Logan said. They want an update on the sanctuary and how we're doing with our expansion program. They've got some questions."

"So it isn't the big hearing." Mary took Sally's cue and reached for the cane propped against the porch railing.

"Ready?" Hank stepped out on the porch and closed the front door behind him. "Hey, Mary. You going to the meeting?"

"No, I don't think I'm invited. Is it open to the public?"

"Interested parties," Hank said. "Come along if you're in that category."

"I am, but I think it's better if I go separately. I was more or less told to stay out of it, but maybe there's some way I can help. Show community support." She turned to Sally and shifted eyeballs only in Hank's direction. "It's more complicated, Sally, so not a word, okay?"

"Of course not. I'm not *that* inappropriate."

"May I keep the pickup awhile longer?"

"It's yours as long as you need it."

It was a small meeting held in a large room, and it was already underway when Mary took advantage of a door left open by a clerk delivering files and followed her into the room. She took a chair close to the door behind a couple of ranchers and an out-of-state bureaucrat—their clothing told their stories—and willed herself fly-on-the-wall status.

Seated on three sides of a square made up of folding tables at the far end on the room were the decision makers. There were three women and two men besides Logan. "Interested parties" occupied a row of folding chairs facing the table. Hank Night Horse sat with Sally and Ann Drexler at one end of the row, and the opposition sat midrow, one man at the center of his own stage. Even with his back to her, Mary could see her father's ruddy face. She could hear his bluster, loud and clear.

"It's about the way we make a living around here," he was saying. "It's not just me. It's a whole way of life. So I've asked Tim Perry—*Senator* Perry—I've asked him to put a hold on transferring the BLM land."

"He can't do that," said one of the committee members. The clerk was circling around behind the participants and handing out papers. "That deal has already been signed, sealed and delivered."

"That's not the way things work in Washington," Tutan said. "You know all that. Tim's been sitting on that crazy ROAM Act for how long now? That piece of legislation would favor the kind of sanctuary you're pushing here. Wide open spaces for a bunch of animals that really don't serve much purpose. I'm not saying get rid of all of them, but let's be sensible. These animals are not indigenous. Not really. And they're not domestic. Can't live with 'em, can't eat 'em." Tutan laughed alone.

"You keep saying *animals,*" Logan said without looking up from the paper he'd been handed. "Is there something wrong with the word *horse?*"

"I like horses. I'm a rancher. The horse is part of my heritage, too."

"He transports you and he does your chores, but he's not a piece of machinery." Logan looked up at Tutan. "And he eats grass."

"That he does." Tutan shifted in his squeaky chair. "My father had a team and wagon. My grandfather used horse-drawn machinery. It's all part of the history books now."

"Along with Indians and cowboys," Logan said.

"It's going to take federal money to keep the Drexlers in business. Nonprofit is business, and they can't tell me otherwise. The way the market is now, that adoption deal has just about priced those horses beyond what anybody with any sense is willing to pay." Tutan wagged a finger. "All it takes is one senator. And I've got mine."

"I don't see any reason to modify the Drexlers' lease at this time," Logan said.

"What about my daughter?"

Logan frowned. "I'm not aware of any Indian land being leased to—"

"She's in on this horse training contest the Drexlers are running. And so are you, Mr. Wolf Track. In fact, you and Mary are in on it together. Partners, right?" Tutan had a couple of committee members' full attention now. "And more. A hell of a lot more. You're *involved* up to your eyeteeth. And that means you have a very personal—"

"I don't know what kind of *personal* relationship you have with Senator Perry, and I don't care. My friendship with Mary has—"

"Careful, Mr. Wolf Track," Tutan said. "Politics is the bread we're feeding on here, and scandal makes the best butter. You know what I'm talking about."

"Don't threaten me, Tutan." Logan's voice was deceptively calm. His eyes would have frozen beer. "This meeting is about lease land, and that's all I intend to discuss with you."

"I increased my bid. In the interest of your own people, you should not have turned it down. I know tribal policy, and I know federal policy. The BIA exists to look after the interests of you Indians."

"The BIA exists to look after the interests of bureaucrats and people like you, Mr. Tutan. But we Indians persevere, and we even try to get along with you. It isn't easy." Logan rose from his chair, his ire bearing down on Mary's father. "Because you have no shame."

The man in charge of the proceedings started up from his chair. "Logan…"

Logan made a palms-up gesture. "Mr. Chairman, I recuse myself from any decision taken today. I don't see any reason to change our position on the leases. Not today, anyway."

"You won't get any argument from me," the chairman said.

"And you haven't heard the last from me," Tutan warned.

Logan spared Mary an angry glance as he left the meeting room. The participants were still talking, but the subject was the next meeting, the next step, the remaining options. *Moving on* was the general sentiment. Tutan wasn't moving, and Mary knew the look on his face without seeing it. He was fuming.

Mary slipped out and found Logan standing outside the front of the building. He gave a nod toward the street corner, and she took his marching orders. They hit the corner shoulder to shoulder, wheeled right and headed for out-of-sight, out-of-mind territory.

"You heard?" he said finally.

"I'm sorry, Logan. I didn't see that coming."

"You could've gotten your story straight with me first."

"Logan…" Keep walking, she told herself. There was no such thing as a good excuse. "There was only the *beginning* of the story and the big leap to conclusions. You don't have to worry, Logan. I'll set the record straight."

"Did I sound worried?" He stopped and turned to her. "Do I look worried?"

"Not at all." She realized they had reached his parked pickup. "You handled it beautifully."

"I can handle any horse they bring me, Mary. A horse's ass is no contest."

Without so much as a fare-thee-well, he got into his pickup and drove away.

Mary read the names on the sides of the boxcars as they rumbled past the front of the pickup. Burlington, Soo, DM&E, Soo, Soo, Soo.

Having no place to go was definitely a downer. She had driven through a major crossroads miles back, watched it shrink appropriately in the rearview mirror. A good turn would have taken her to her best friend's place. A terrible turn would have led to the house she'd grown up in and most of the clothes she'd brought with her. A hundred and eighty degree turn would have headed her toward the home of the man she loved. *Yes, loved.* But she'd kept right on gunning her internal and external engines, tooling down the road, imagining a clean bed in a small-town motel and telling herself everything would be fine. Another week and she would be a plane ride away from a life in good order. She'd have her calendar on the wall and a clock in every room. She would get back to work with her dogs, and she would be fine.

She patted her stomach. "*We'll* be fine."

Be happy, her mother had said.

"I want to be happy," Mary whispered. *Clackity clackity-clackity.* "It's going to be slim pickings at lullaby time, kid. Mama knows the words, but can't sing." But she found a melancholy tune in her sparse repertoire—or it found her—and she hummed it as the train trailed down the tracks. She wanted to sing happily, be happy, make happiness happen with the one—the ones—she loved.

The South Dakota sun dove off the edge of a butte and splashed chokecherry juice all over the evening sky. Mary's mind's eye called up an image of lodge poles and camp smoke and the silhouette of a clay-bank horse. It was a scene she could only dream if she ever found that motel bed.

She put the pickup in reverse. She owed herself the real thing for one more night.

The tipi glowed from the inside out like a small table lamp in a child's bedroom decorated with cowboys and Indians. A change from making the campfire outside, Mary thought. Maybe he felt as cold as he'd looked with his parting glance.

She hadn't expected company at the campsite. She hadn't expected *to be* company. But she wasn't turning around again, not tonight. If he turned her away, she'd sleep in a pickup bed, which was about on par with what she could have rented in a one-motel town. She was a soldier, after all, and a bed was a bed unless it had a canopy of stars. Then it was God's gift to the restive soul.

"First lesson, little one. The stars belong to everyone." Mary started in humming again, working up the nerve to announce herself at the tipi door. She'd read the chapter on tipi protocol in the book Mother had quoted to her about Crazy Horse. They hadn't called it *protocol,* of course. But they hadn't said anything about a code, either.

Adobe nickered to her from the round pen. *Me first.* Mary smiled against the twilight stillness as she turned on her heel. There was order, and then there was natural order.

"What do you call it, boy? You know where you stand, but you wouldn't say 'pecking order'." She gave the thick black mane a finger raking. "What was that sound you made, hmm? What do you call me?"

She heard her partner coming. She would know him anywhere by the rhythm of his footsteps. It was a realization at once startling and soothing, and she embraced it, filing it away with others of its kind. She'd never loved this way before, and it was unsettling.

"What do you want to be called?" Logan asked as he took possession of the top fence rail with merely a hand. "Say I'm the peck*er.* Are you here to play peck*ee?*"

She laughed without turning to him. His voice sounded even richer in the dark than it did in daylight.

"But that's just us," he said. "Our boy's social life defies name-calling. He knows who he is, and now that he's got us figured out, he's ready to write the book. Only trouble is, he's got no use for labels." He laid his forearms along the rail and stacked his fists to make a pillow for his chin. "You can't write the book without labels, fella. And a hook. You gotta have a hook."

"*Pecker* and *peckee* sounds pretty catchy," Mary said. The coarse horsehair felt cool and substantial between her fingers.

"Does it work for you? It's mostly women who buy the horse books."

"What works for me is…*what works*. I'm suspicious of hooks and lines. I don't care if you have a string of letters after your name. I want to read about what you've done."

"You mean, with horses?"

"Isn't that what you're writing about?"

"I'm not writing anything right now. I'm courting."

"Seriously?"

He hooked his elbow over the fence and angled toward her. "You're out here talkin' to a horse, and you're asking if *I'm* serious?"

"You talk to them all the time."

"They're good listeners. Not too many people appreciate that, but you do. Which is why I'm asking you what you want to be called." He reached out to tuck her hair behind her ear. "And not by the horse you rode in on. By the man you came here to see."

"I came looking for a bed. I didn't expect to find a man."

"Don't lie to me, woman."

"I was looking for a motel," she amended. "But I had to stop for a train that was pulling a string of boxcars from every station east of the Missouri."

"And that gave you some time to think." Smiling wistfully, the angles of his face softened by rosy shadows, he traced her jaw line with the backs of his fingers, earlobe to chin. "And you thought to yourself, 'Now where would Logan be tonight?'"

"I thought, 'If I could sleep anywhere in the world tonight, where would it be?'"

"I can't invite you in unless you tell me what to call you."

"Not baby. Not—"

"What do you want me to call you?" he insisted, teasing the corner of her mouth with his thumb. "And how many times a day?"

"I thought my name was the plainest in the world until I heard you say it."

"Mary." He slid his fingers into her hair, pressed her nape and drew her into his gentle kiss. "Mary," he whispered against her lips and kissed her again.

"Mary." He took her in his arms and kissed her worries and wishes in two directions, past and future. Everything she wanted was there for her in the moment.

They made love outside the tipi under the stars. He touched her so tenderly she wanted to cry, treated her body like a precious vessel, one that held wonderful secrets and sacred dreams. In his hands she was not herself. She was more than Mary. She was Mary on fire, Mary undone, done over, done completely and thoroughly and right. She was Mary at home with Logan.

They lay together in his blankets—courting robes, he called them—and counted the features they admired about each other, seen and unseen. They spoke of pleasure, his and hers, and how it came about and how it flowed between them and thrummed throughout even now, but softly. Soft as the night.

"I promised myself I wouldn't ask again," he ventured, his voice deep and deliberate. "And I don't make a habit of breaking my promises. I don't make a habit of leaving my clothes on the floor or getting hammered on Friday night, either, but that doesn't mean I haven't done it."

"I have to go back to Fort Hood," she said, anticipating the question.

"I know."

"I told my mother, and I told Sally about the pregnancy. They both assumed…"

"That I'm the baby's father?" She nodded cheek to shoulder, skin to skin. "And you said…"

"I didn't get a chance to explain." She closed her eyes. "I didn't want to."

"Then don't. They're not coming at you with DNA kits."

She was quietly amused. "I can tell you right now, this baby won't look anything like you."

"You've met my sons. Do they have their father's eyes?" He propped himself up on his elbow, and she tucked her arm beneath her head where his shoulder had been. "I just made love to you. You made love to me. I *assume* that's where babies come from."

"You are the most beautiful man I've ever—"

"Stop saying that, and just tell me what I need to hear."

"I love you." She pushed up, hooked her arm behind his head and kissed him. Then she pressed her forehead against his and closed her eyes. "I love you. I love you. I love you."

"That's a start."

She looked up at him. "I don't know when I can come back, Logan. And I know if I do—*when* I do— well, you called it. My father—who hates horses—is a horse's ass."

"Then I guess I won't be offering him horses in return for his daughter's hand." He smiled. "You think he'd take a used pickup?"

"I know he'd take the shirt off your back."

"That's your job." He urged her back down with a kiss, and then hovered over, stroking her hair, his eyes taking in each feature of her face as though he were planning to duplicate her somehow. "How many nights do we have before you have to go?" He chuckled. "I suppose I'll have to get a calendar, huh?"

"And a code."

"I've got a code." He laid his hand over breast and tapped in time with her heartbeat. "I-do. Love-you. I-do. Love-you."

"Not enough," she whispered. "Not enough nights. Not enough days."

"How many do you need?" His hand stilled, but it stayed in position. Or possession. "People get married before they get deployed all the time. You know that better than I do. And they have babies, and then get deployed. They love each other, they make it work."

"Some do. Some fall apart."

"Look, Mary, I don't have letters after my name or a rank in front of it. But you know what I've done. And you know how I feel." He grinned. "And you're no spring chicken, either."

"What?"

"You're not a kid. We're not gonna fall apart. It is what it is, and we'll make the best of it."

"I hate that expression. *It is what it is.*"

"Until it changes." He rolled to his back and lay

beside her. "You get married, you make a promise, and it's 'for better, for worse.' It's not *or.* It's *'and.'* Everybody gets both."

"How long were you together? You and…" Overhead, the stars danced, mocking her.

"I wasn't watching the clock. All I know is, the older you get, the longer your tale. The more kinks, the more knots, the more twists. But who wants a plain ol' straight one? How boring is that?"

She laughed. "How are you spelling this tale?"

"I'm not." He took her hand in his and held it between their hips, as though they were marching hand in hand toward the stars.

"Well, what kind are we talking about?"

"Any kind you want." He gave her hand a quick squeeze. "You want a bedtime story? You want a tiger in your tank? I can give you either, or."

"Both. I want the *and.* I can make it through the worse, and I can always do better." She drew his hand to her flat belly. "Are you sure you want us?"

"You know me, Mary. If I wasn't sure, I wouldn't ask."

"I know you." She stroked the back of his hand. "You're one of a kind."

"What kind is that?"

"My kind."

Epilogue

The two men sat side by side on a bench beside the door marked Judge's Chambers. Elbows on their knees, Stetsons taking up space between calves, brims occupying restless fingers, they would have made a handsome pair of bookends.

Logan had felt underdressed when he saw that Hank had worn a tie, but Hank had already taken it off, rolled it up and stuffed it in his pocket, and they'd both been tugging at their crisp white collars. The early morning air felt good against a clammy neck. But if the women didn't hurry, the sport coats would soon be hitting the bench.

Hank straightened up first. "Are you ready for this, man?"

"Oh yeah, definitely." But he'd sure be glad when the formalities were over. He planted the heel of a hand on his knee and pushed up slowly. "Are you?"

"I've been ready. I owe you one for hitching up the bandwagon. I thought Sally would never quit hemmin' and hawin' around. But, hell, this works for me. Annie and Zach had a fancy affair at a lodge in the Black Hills." Hank put his hat on. "It was nice."

"This will be nice. Short and sweet."

Hank nodded. "And you know Texas isn't too far away. I've driven it many times. I can make it down to Austin in sixteen, seventeen hours."

"I could make it in two if I could fly direct, but you gotta go west or east first. Makes no sense." Logan clapped his hat on his head and gave a dry chuckle. "Maybe I'll hire a chopper and rap jump onto the parade grounds. She'd get a kick out of that."

"You could ride down on that little mustang. He'd sure be saddle broke by the time you got there. For my money, nothing beats a good endurance horse."

"I thought it was Zach's rich brother's money you guys were giving away."

"Yep, Sam put up the prize money. He's helped out a lot with the sanctuary." Hank tipped his head to the side and ran a finger between his neck and collar. "Yeah, he's a good man, that Sam Beaudry."

"Anybody can bid on the horses after the competition is over, right?"

Hank nodded. "We expect the winner to go pretty high."

"Mary loves that horse. I want to give him to her. She's the one signed up for the contest, but Adobe isn't hers. I could get him for her."

"You're supposed to give the horse to her father."

"Her father doesn't care too much for horses. Or family." Logan glanced toward the courthouse entrance. *Come on, door.* "Another good reason for going the short and sweet route."

"Maybe the best. Every time Damn Tootin opens his mouth around me, my fist itches to shut it for him."

Logan smiled. "Hey, man, you're supposed to be a healer."

"Yeah, well, the guy's been a burr under my saddle for a long time, and I can't think of a better cure for that particular itch. Like they say, physician's assistant, heal thyself."

The laugh they shared stopped abruptly. The front door opened, and Zach Beaudry appeared, tossing a quick grin to the grooms in waiting. The bookends pulled their hats off and rose from the bench in tandem as Zach pulled the door back, doffed his black Stetson, and gave a deferential gesture. "Ladies."

Each was lovely in her own right. Ann and Audrey wore pink corsages and bright-eyed smiles. From rubber tip to curved handle Sally's cane sported a blooming vine with flowers to match the sassy red rose she'd tucked behind her ear.

And then along came Mary. Logan's Mary. He had never seen her much-loved body decked out in a dress and high heels, and the sight of her took his breath away. An elbow in the side urged him to inhale, but he waited until she reached him, took his arm and filled his nose with the scent of roses and morning and Mary.

"You look beautiful," he whispered.

"So do you." Her soft pink mouth turned up at the corners. Her blue eyes glittered like water in sunshine. Logan wanted to dive in.

But instead he offered his arm and led the way into the judge's chambers, where two marriages were made with promises, kisses and names signed on solid lines.

"Honeymoon time," Ann announced after bussing her sister's cheek. She took Mary's weepy mother by the arm. "Audrey's coming with us. You kids have fun. Send postcards."

As Mary rushed to give her mother one more kiss, she overheard her husband—*her husband*—ask someone, "Are you taking a trip?"

"Not until Mustang Sally's Makeover Challenge is over," Hank answered. "I found us a bridal suite in Rapid City, but all she'll give me is one night."

"One night away from home," Sally amended.

"After that, well..." She waved their marriage license under Hank's nose. "I've got your signature now, cowboy. I hope you read the fine print. Even if we get the ROAM Act passed, it won't apply to you."

"Unless I'm working."

"Workin' ain't roamin', honey." Sally turned to Logan. "Where are you two headed?"

"That's their business, woman." Hank gave a jerk of his chin in the direction of the paper in his wife's hand. "According to that fine print, you've got a husband to tend to."

"Hoo-wee!" Sally punched the air with her licensed hand. "Let the tending begin."

Mary buckled her seat belt and arranged the flimsy fabric of her new dress over her knees. As always, Sally had left a palpable silence behind her. Mary wanted Logan to speak first. She wondered what he would say. Something about being happy. If she said it first, it wouldn't be quite the same. Mentally she put words into his head and willed them to come out of his mouth. Not *exactly*—she wanted them to be his words put together his way—but something to the effect that he was happy.

But she broke her silence when he missed the turn to Sinte.

"Where are we going? I didn't bring anything with me. I thought we'd be going to your place."

Eyes on the road, he smiled. "We're going to your place."

Her place?

He took a familiar turn, and she smiled, too. Camp was her place. She could think of no better way to spend a honeymoon than sleeping under South Dakota skies with her new husband. She was married. She'd said yes, I'll marry Wolf Track, and suddenly she was Mary Wolf Track. Signing it for the first time had felt surprisingly right. *Mary Wolf Track.*

It had pleased him, too. She'd seen it in his eyes.

Adobe welcomed them with raised head and alert ears. Logan must have brought him out before first light. He had this planned.

"Here we are," he said as he shut off the ignition. "Mary's place. No curtains to hang. No floors to scrub. The other warriors will be army-green with envy."

"And they won't let me join in their warrior games."

"Good. Pregnant women can't be warriors."

He left her to ponder that one, but by the time he'd come around to open the passenger door, she had an answer. "Maybe not in your world."

"You just married into my world. In my world, the tipi belongs to the woman. I can either give you my horses or my pickup to carry it in." He took a pointed look at her insubstantial shoes and lifted her off the seat and into his arms, across-the-threshold style. "Wedding present."

"Haven't I read somewhere that you're supposed to give the horses to my father?"

"Damn. That man doesn't let go even when he's not around. Your father only gets horses if we're going to pitch your new tipi beside his. You want to be part of his *tiospaye?*"

"No!"

She hugged his neck and laughed. Her laugh started small, but when he joined in, it became uproarious.

"You know what it means?"

"Doesn't matter."

"Part of his herd."

"No."

"Part of his cattle empire."

"No."

"Part of his legacy."

"No, no, no!"

They were still laughing when he set her on her feet beside the round pen, each with an arm still around the other. The mustang trotted over to their side of the circle, undoubtedly wondering what was so funny.

"She looks pretty, doesn't she, 'Dobe?" Logan held his hand out, inviting a sniff. "Yeah, I put the clothes we brought for her in the lodge. We won't be carrying her around all day."

"I'll go in and change," Mary said. "What are we going to teach him today?"

"I'm thinking we ought to take him out of the competition."

Stunned, Mary looked up at her new husband. "Why?"

Logan lifted one shoulder. "With you gone, his heart won't be in it."

"*His* heart?"

"Mine will be with you, but I need his to be involved in the work." He looked into her eyes. He was serious. "Let me adopt him."

"I was hoping you'd say that." She pressed her cheek to his shoulder. "About the baby."

"You're my wife." He reached down and laid his free hand on the lowest part of her belly. "I've been inside you, Mary. I'm your husband, and I belong here. The child growing here is my child. Put my name on the birth certificate."

"Is that legal?"

"It is if you say it is. But I'm good with adoption, too, if that's what you want. *Hunka,* we call it. We have a ceremony—you have paperwork. Either way, I become a father."

"I love you so much, Logan." She turned to him fully, arms around him, face tucked against the side of his neck. He smelled like man, spice and sunshine. "Will you be with me when the baby's born?"

"You know I will."

She lifted her face so she could see his dark eyes. "Wild horses won't keep you away?"

"Neither will guards at the gate." His kiss was a gentle promise. "I'll go to you whenever I can, and you'll come home to me. Lots of people live that way these days."

"Not us. I've served long enough to qualify for a voluntary separation and an honorable discharge. I'm going to start the paperwork when I get back."

"Are you sure that's what you want?"

"I can still train dogs. I don't have to give that up." She smiled. "I'm sure I want to be with my husband."

"How long before I get you back?"

"Not long." She closed her eyes. "But it's going to feel like forever."

"If they don't want to let you out, I'm going in after you."

"Commando?"

His eyes twinkled. "What do you think?"

"I think you're in for a professional pat down, Wolf Track."

And her hand on his shoulder started its descent.

* * * * *

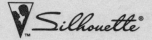
Silhouette®

COMING NEXT MONTH
Available September 28, 2010

#2071 A COLD CREEK BABY
RaeAnne Thayne
The Cowboys of Cold Creek

#2072 WHEN THE COWBOY SAID "I DO"
Crystal Green
Montana Mavericks: Thunder Canyon Cowboys

#2073 ADDING UP TO MARRIAGE
Karen Templeton
Wed in the West

#2074 CADE COULTER'S RETURN
Lois Faye Dyer
Big Sky Brothers

#2075 ROYAL HOLIDAY BABY
Leanne Banks

#2076 NOT JUST THE NANNY
Christie Ridgway

SPECIAL EDITION

REQUEST YOUR FREE BOOKS!

2 FREE NOVELS PLUS 2 FREE GIFTS!

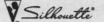

SPECIAL EDITION
Life, Love and Family!

YES! Please send me 2 FREE Silhouette® Special Edition® novels and my 2 FREE gifts (gifts are worth about \$10). After receiving them, if I don't wish to receive any more books, I can return the shipping statement marked "cancel." If I don't cancel, I will receive 6 brand-new novels every month and be billed just \$4.24 per book in the U.S. or \$4.99 per book in Canada. That's a saving of 15% off the cover price! It's quite a bargain! Shipping and handling is just 50¢ per book.* I understand that accepting the 2 free books and gifts places me under no obligation to buy anything. I can always return a shipment and cancel at any time. Even if I never buy another book from Silhouette, the two free books and gifts are mine to keep forever.

235/335 SDN E5RG

Name	(PLEASE PRINT)	
Address		Apt. #
City	State/Prov.	Zip/Postal Code

Signature (if under 18, a parent or guardian must sign)

Mail to the **Silhouette Reader Service:**
IN U.S.A.: P.O. Box 1867, Buffalo, NY 14240-1867
IN CANADA: P.O. Box 609, Fort Erie, Ontario L2A 5X3

Not valid for current subscribers to Silhouette Special Edition books.

Want to try two free books from another line?
Call 1-800-873-8635 or visit www.morefreebooks.com.

* Terms and prices subject to change without notice. Prices do not include applicable taxes. N.Y. residents add applicable sales tax. Canadian residents will be charged applicable provincial taxes and GST. Offer not valid in Quebec. This offer is limited to one order per household. All orders subject to approval. Credit or debit balances in a customer's account(s) may be offset by any other outstanding balance owed by or to the customer. Please allow 4 to 6 weeks for delivery. Offer available while quantities last.

Your Privacy: Silhouette is committed to protecting your privacy. Our Privacy Policy is available online at www.eHarlequin.com or upon request from the Reader Service. From time to time we make our lists of customers available to reputable third parties who may have a product or service of interest to you. If you would prefer we not share your name and address, please check here. ☐

Help us get it right—We strive for accurate, respectful and relevant communications. To clarify or modify your communication preferences, visit us at www.ReaderService.com/consumerschoice.

SSE10R

*See below for a sneak peek at
our inspirational line, Love Inspired®.
Introducing HIS HOLIDAY BRIDE
by bestselling author Jillian Hart*

Autumn Granger gave her horse rein to slide toward the town's new sheriff.

"Hey, there." The man in a brand-new Stetson, black T-shirt, jeans and riding boots held up a hand in greeting. He stepped away from his four-wheel drive with "Sheriff" in black on the doors and waded through the grasses. "I'm new around here."

"I'm Autumn Granger."

"Nice to meet you, Miss Granger. I'm Ford Sherman, from Chicago." He knuckled back his hat, revealing the most handsome face she'd ever seen. Big blue eyes contrasted with his sun-tanned complexion.

"I'm guessing you haven't seen much open land. Out here, you've got to keep an eye on cows or they're going to tear your vehicle apart."

"What?" He whipped around. Sure enough, mammoth black-and-white creatures had started to gnaw on his four-wheel drive. They clustered like a mob, mouths and tongues and teeth bent on destruction. One cow tried to pry the wiper off the windshield, another chewed on the side mirror. Several leaned through the open window, licking the seats.

"Move along, little dogie." He didn't know the first thing about cattle.

The entire herd swiveled their heads to study him curiously. Not a single hoof shifted. The animals soon returned to chewing, licking, digging through his possessions.

Autumn laughed, a warm and wonderful sound. "Thanks,

I needed that." She then pulled a bag from behind her saddle and waved it at the cows. "Look what I have, guys. Cookies."

Cows swung in her direction, and dozens of liquid brown eyes brightened with cookie hopes. As she circled the car, the cattle bounded after her. The earth shook with the force of their powerful hooves.

"Next time, you're on your own, city boy." She tipped her hat. The cowgirl stayed on his mind, the sweetest thing he had ever seen.

*Will Ford be able to stick it out in the country
to find out more about Autumn?
Find out in HIS HOLIDAY BRIDE
by bestselling author Jillian Hart,
available in October 2010
only from Love Inspired®.*